ENDORSEMENTS

M000318312

"In *An Unclouded Day*, Christian novelist Ramona Bridges has delivered her best thus far, crossing the lines of a variety of genres...Her characters are both complex and true-to-life, and the narrative and dialogue accurately portray the realities of both place and time in rural MS in the early 1900's...not only a pleasurable read but a real page-turner as well." – Glenn Shoemake, Okatoma Literary Guild

"*An Unclouded Day* ends Ramona Bridges' "story about love" trilogy – a sad day for the fans who enjoy spending time with her well-developed characters, now our friends. Like The Help by Stockett, this is a story that is dear to our hearts and a story that will endure the test of time." – Mary Emrick, owner, Turning Pages Books & More, Natchez, MS

"Ramona is adept at painting mental pictures with words, allowing the reader to see the story in vivid detail...As I read *An Unclouded Day*, at times I found myself walking right alongside the characters, weeping with them in their sorrow, rejoicing with them in their joy. I particularly like that each chapter is introduced with a verse of Scripture that offers reassurance and guidance for the situation therein." – Bro. Harold Ishee, pastor, Laurel, MS

"*An Unclouded Day* is truly a diverse work of historic fiction... the characters and places come to life with long-forgotten Southern dialect that conjures memories of the old South, but most importantly, it is a story of family and infallible faith." – Patsy Brewer, Library Director, Waynesboro-Wayne Co. Library, Waynesboro, MS

"The story, the characters, and the lives of this family continue to intrigue as mystery after mystery unfolds...Ramona Bridges has given her readers an unforgettable story." – Jean H. Holifield, co-owner WBBN Radio Station, Laurel, MS

"Ramona has the wonderful ability of speaking to places in the readers' hearts and drawing them right into every scene. Her 'story about love' series has all the ingredients of a great family saga. *An Unclouded Day* is the crowning jewel to this delightful trilogy." – Jo Jefcoat Hubbard, Mt Olive, MS

"*An Unclouded Day* is a poignant look at the intricacies of life in the early 1900's in rural Mississippi. Through her masterful use of words, Ramona brings her characters to life and transports her readers back to that simpler time. I am sorry to see this series end." – Mona Swayze, South MS Regional Library System

"*Sweet By and By, Standing On the Promises, An Unclouded Day*...You will find yourself re-reading this trilogy time and again just to revisit people you have grown to love...Kudos to Ramona!" – Charlotte Myrick, owner, Baptist Bible and Book House, Laurel, MS

"More surprises and secrets revealed...a wonderful final chapter to the Addie saga!" – Kay McQueen, Collins, MS

The Warren-Coulter-Graham Family

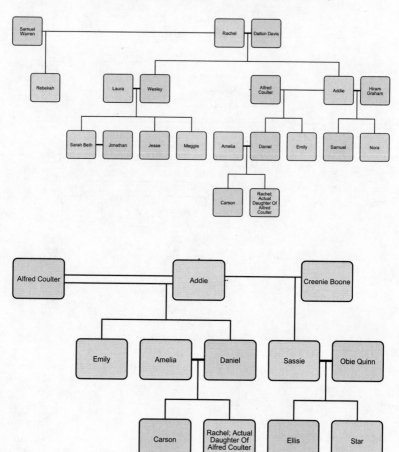

The Bradleys

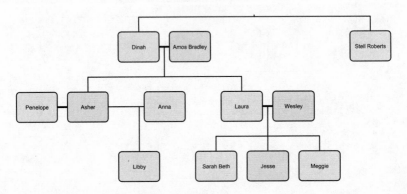

the grace of our Lord
Jesus Christ be with you —
Ramona Bridges

AN UNCLOUDED DAY

RAMONA BRIDGES

AN UNCLOUDED DAY

A story about love

sequel to

SWEET BY AND BY

and

STANDING ON THE PROMISES

TATE PUBLISHING
AND ENTERPRISES, LLC

An Unclouded Day
Copyright © 2013 by Ramona Bridges. All rights reserved.

No part of this publication may be reproduced, stored in a retrieval system or transmitted in any way by any means, electronic, mechanical, photocopy, recording or otherwise without the prior permission of the author except as provided by USA copyright law.

The opinions expressed by the author are not necessarily those of Tate Publishing, LLC.

Published by Tate Publishing & Enterprises, LLC
127 E. Trade Center Terrace | Mustang, Oklahoma 73064 USA
1.888.361.9473 | www.tatepublishing.com

Tate Publishing is committed to excellence in the publishing industry. The company reflects the philosophy established by the founders, based on Psalm 68:11,
"The Lord gave the word and great was the company of those who published it."

Book design copyright © 2013 by Tate Publishing, LLC. All rights reserved.
Cover design by Rtor Maghuyop
Interior design by Jomel Pepito

Published in the United States of America

ISBN: 978-1-62854-865-5
1. FICTION / Christian / Historical
2. FICTION / Christian / Romance
13.09.11

TRIBUTE AND DEDICATION

*F*ound among her personal papers years after her death, the poem entitled "Mabel Claire" found in chapter 5 of this book was penned by my great-grandmother Mabel Robertson-Knight, on August 14, 1906. It is truly a blessing and an honor for me to have had the unique opportunity of interweaving this work of hers into the storyline of *An Unclouded Day*.

This book is dedicated in memory of her.

LIST OF CHARACTERS

(OF TRILOGY)

1. Addie Coulter-Graham: heroine of series; daughter of Samuel and Rachel Warren, and Dalton Davis; wife of Alfred; second wife of Hiram.

2. Alfred Coulter: villain of *Sweet By and By*, first husband of Addie, murderer and rapist.

3. Hiram Graham: second husband of Addie.

4. Wesley Warren: brother of Addie, husband of Laura Bradley.

5. Claire Ellis: beloved friend of Addie, wife of Luke.

6. Daniel Coulter: son of Alfred and Addie, husband of Amelia.

7. Amelia Rose Riley-Coulter: daughter of Pete and Bonnie Riley, wife of Daniel.

8. Emily Victoria Coulter: daughter of Alfred and Addie.

9. Sassie Boone: illegitimate daughter of Creenie Boone and Alfred Coulter.

10. Dorethea "Dorrie" Boone: auntie of Creenie and Sassie.

11. Dr. Travis Hughes: the town's doctor, husband of Abigail Langford.

12. Amos and Dinah Bradley: parents of twins Asher and Laura.

13. Stell Roberts: cantankerous surrogate mother of Asher and Laura Bradley; she shared a house with Claire Ellis.

14. Anna Bradley: first wife of Asher, mother of Libby.

15. Ap Carver: Claire's friend and handyman.

16. Cleve Walls: field hand.

17. Sarah Beth, Jesse, and Meggie Warren: children of Wesley and Laura.

18. Jennie Grayson: Amelia's aunt.

19. Gent: Alfred Coulter's horse.

20. Ben: Daniel Coulter's hound.

21. Bernice Crowley: schoolteacher.

22. John-Ott and Leah Owens: proprietors of the restaurant the Preacher's House.

23. Jonathan Langford: banker, husband of Sarah Beth, brother of Abigail.

24. Maude Thorne: organist for Harmony Baptist Church.

25. Rev. J. D. Higgins: preacher of Harmony Baptist Church.

26. Wilkes Graham: villain of *Standing On The Promises* and *An Unclouded Day*, brother of Hiram.

27. Ezra and Rosette Quinn: parents of Obie and Etta, in-laws of Sassie.

28. Obie Quinn: husband of Sassie, father of Ellis and Star.

29. Beulah Quinn: Ezra's sister-in-law.

30. Georgianne Knight: mute sister of Rosette Quinn.

31. Libby Bradley: daughter of Asher and Anna, stepdaughter of Penelope.

32. Dr. Stephen Alexander: Libby's psychiatrist, husband of Miranda.

33. Louella Stinson: prostitute who lives with Wilkes Graham.

34. Rachel and Carson Coulter: children of Daniel and Amelia.

35. Samuel and Nora Graham: children of Hiram and Addie.

36. Dalton Davis: real father of Wesley and Addie.

37. Rebekah: deceased daughter of Samuel and Rachel.

38. Charlotte Davis-Adams: sister of Dalton Davis, aunt of Wesley and Addie.

39. Claudia: Charlotte Adams's housekeeper and cook.

40. Matt and Julie Robertson: parents of Mabel Claire "Belle" Robertson.

PROLOGUE

*H*er lungs bursting, fourteen-year-old Libby Bradley crashed through a hedge thicket in the dense bottomland along Cedar Creek, about a half-mile upstream from her house. Limbs hit her sharply across the face, stinging like a leather whip; the fanglike thorns of a saw briar attacked her neck and arms. Gasping for breath, she stumbled and almost fell when her feet became entangled in the woody cordage of a rambling grapevine. Her legs hurt from running so hard; her shins burned like they were on fire. Tired as she was though, she knew she couldn't slow down. She had to keep running.

In a mindless panic, she pushed on, like a hunted animal, weaving a frantic zigzagging course through dogwoods and sweet gums and hickory trees. As she ran, she lost all awareness of time. She had no idea how long she had been running when she first came to realize that a deep hush had settled over the woods. The silence was so profound it seemed almost mystical. No birds tweeted, no squirrels barked, no twigs cracked. The only sounds she heard were the wild pounding of her own heart and the sound of the man running behind her, chasing her. She didn't dare look back to see how close he was, but his footfalls were growing louder and louder. She could tell he was gaining on her.

With young strength ebbing, raw fear surged through her. Not knowing what else to do, in a small voice she began reciting the prayer her daddy had taught her when she was a little girl: "Now I lay me down to sleep, I pray the Lord my soul to keep. If I should die before I wake, I pray the Lord my soul to take."

CHAPTER 1

I thank my God upon every remembrance of you…

*—Philippians 1:3 (*KJV*)*

 t was after the turn of the century, the year 1906, a year
that promised boundless opportunity and good fortune to
many. Harvard University graduate Theodore "Teddy" Roosevelt
was the twenty-sixth president of the United States. A prominent
businessman named John D. Rockefeller was one of the country's
first multimillionaires, having made his fortune in oil refining
and the railroad, and the Vanderbilts, respectively, in the shipping
industry. In Chicago, Montgomery "Monkey" Wards and Sears,
Roebuck and Company competed for the mail-order catalogue
primacy, and in many major cities across the land, the invention
of electricity and telephones gave cause to marvel; Michigan-
born Henry Ford had constructed the first horseless carriage and
was nurturing an incredibly ambitious idea of someday mass-
producing a gas-powered vehicle he had designed, called a car.
There were airplanes and ocean liners traversing the globe.

However, for all the progress and prosperity among the affluent well-to-dos, America was still a predominately rural country and the aforementioned facts and events had little bearing on the day-to-day strife and struggles of the common folk, pointedly for those living in and around the small town of Oakdale, Mississippi, and the surrounding community of Golden Meadow.

Most folks there had not yet seen a gleaming porcelain tub or a paved street, much less an electric cable car. Rooms were still lit by candles and kerosene, water still drawn from a well and heated on a woodstove, and in most every backyard stood a smelly outhouse. Here, there was much work to be done year-round just to survive, and people lived poor. Families were sacred, neighbor helped neighbor, and the Sabbath Day was kept and remembered.

"Girl, why you be lookin' up 'side my head all crazy?" Rosette asked, as though she didn't know.

Every year, usually in March and October, a group of twenty or more women from Mt. Zion Church met up with hoes, rakes, shears, and brushes to groom the church grounds and tend the graves. Customarily, they made a day of it, packing picnic hampers and working until daylight gave out. Today's dinner fare consisted of cold fried chicken, potato salad, pickled okra, pickled cucumbers and peaches, watermelon-rind preserves, and lemonade.

They had picked a good day for it. It was shady and not too hot; the scent of roses, still in late bloom, sweetened the air and would until frost bit them back.

For the last hour, sisters Rosette Quinn and Georgianne Knight had been working a plot alongside each other, nattering back and forth the entire time, as was their way. They, in fact, in years past, had, or at least fancied themselves to have, reason enough to despise each other. It was not until only three years ago that they had come face-to-face again and resumed speaking, after a long-standing estrangement that had kept them from each other's company for nearly two decades—during which time Georgianne, the town's potter, had gone so far as to pass herself off as being mute.

"You da one be crazy, you crazy ol' fool," Georgianne huffed.

"What I say?"

"Talkin' 'bout how you don't know why Obie an' Sassie jus' won't come live wif yaw. Hmmph!" Georgianne adjusted her straw hat. "Same reason I wouldn't."

"I don't remember ever axin' *you*." Rosette arched her back, making her bones snap.

"An' you needn't ever either. You'z too mean an' bossy, jus' like—who dat mean man in da Bible dey say kilt all dem chi'ren an' John da Baptist? King Herod, uh-huh, dat who!"

Rosette pursed her lips. "All I say wuz how I could be a help to da girl, look after Ellis an' Baby Star when Sassie be out in da field an' such."

"See. Dat jus' what I be talkin' 'bout. Bossy! You done took it on yo' bossy self to put *Sassie* out in da field." Georgianne was almost out of breath from wrestling with a clump of crabgrass. "Why yo' big, black butt cain't be out in da field *an' such* an' she be lookin' after her *own* chi'ren? I knows why, jus' like dey knows why. Now yo' girl Etta done jumped da broom an' lef', you be lookin' fo' somebody to move in an' wait on you hoof an' paw." She tugged at the grass harder. "Nex' thang po' Sassie know, she be totin' all da water, washin' all da clothes, cookin' all da meals—"

Rosette interrupted her with, "When you finally die, I done got a place picked out fo' you, right over dere by dat fence"— she pointed with her trowel—"right beside da dust of ol' Hilmer Clayton, craziest, stinkin'est ol' heathen ever to walk da face o' da earth. Yaw be perfect fo' each other, live or dead!"

Georgianne snorted. "I ain't plannin' to leave here 'til least a hun'red-twenty. Time I dies, worms'll done have yo' rickety ol' bones picked clean as God's fangernails." The roots of the crabgrass finally turned loose.

At that precise moment, from across the cemetery, somebody hollered, "Yaw gittin' hungry? Come on now an' let's eat!"

With the help of her rake, Georgianne stood up, presenting her back to Rosette.

Poking her firmly on the backside with her hoe handle, Rosette remarked, "Mighty big talk fo' somebody wif such a bony lil' hinny." She, on the other hand, could walk to town and back with a bowl of peas balanced on her plump rump, and not waste a one.

As a parting gibe, Georgianne said, as though to herself, "Like da mens say, ain't always da biggest berries dat make da sweetest jam." Grinning at her own audacity and unconcerned about how ridiculous she looked, she walked toward the table with a prissy mince, imitating the movements of a sashaying Southern belle.

Whereas the comical display provoked all the other women to laugh raucously, Rosette could but stare after her sister in wordless disdain.

Anyone traveling along Longview Road would most certainly have taken pause to appreciate Hiram and Addie Graham's place, not that it was by any means palatial or grandiose—except to those who lived there—but rather for the pervading sense of peacefulness it evoked.

Set a short distance off the road, surrounded by oaks and magnolias, the house itself was built of cypress. Rustic in both design and setting, it looked like it had been there since Solomon's Temple. The woodshed and smokehouse in the backyard and the barn and woodshop beyond the garden were of the same weathered gray as the house.

Married to each other for seven years, Hiram and Addie both had endured and survived previous spouses. Addie had two children by her first husband, Alfred Coulter: a grown son named Daniel and a daughter, Emily, age seventeen. While Hiram's first marriage had yielded no children, he and Addie had a son, age six, named Samuel, after her father; and a two-year-old daughter, Nora, named for Hiram's late mother.

Although their youth had passed, their love and respect for each other had flourished and grown more solid, deeper, over the years. And whereby there had never been a woman less aware of her physical attractiveness than Addie, at forty-one, she was still a pretty woman—one of the prettiest women Hiram had ever known, and far prettier to him now than he remembered her ever being before.

Hiram and Daniel had not tarried over the noontime meal, nor had Addie expected they would. And ordinarily, Nora would have eaten with them at the kitchen table, but Laura had come to visit awhile ago, and Addie had let her walk home with her aunt, as she often did. Being the youngest of the children in the family, Nora was everyone's darling, and she got to play with everyone's toys, especially when school was in. She would entertain herself for hours at Laura's, playing with Meggie's old dolls.

When Addie had cleared away the dishes and spread a cloth over the leftover food, she poured the last cup of coffee and went out onto the front porch. She knew the landscape before her in every season, and as she looked out across it now, she likened the scene to a painting limned on canvas, yet unfinished. The first splotches of russet, mauve, and gold marked the meadow and the wood line beyond, signifying that autumn was upon them, even though the days were still warm. She surmised it would only be a short matter of time before it would be too chilly to leave the windows open at night, not long until they would again be sleeping under heavy quilts.

As she stood looking, a peculiar feeling came over her, a longing almost. Though she did not know why, something about this time of year—the changing colors, a particular smell in the air, a vague taste on the tongue—all these came together into some intangible something that brought on this certain feeling. It was ineffable, one she couldn't describe, and one that no one could understand unless they experienced it themselves. Whatever it was, it made her spirit ache with a sort of melancholy and made her feel lonesome, grievous even. *It makes me miss Claire*, she thought. Though Claire had been gone for almost four years, Addie still missed her more than words could say... and if she closed her eyes, she could almost believe she was still there with her, as it seemed she had always been.

Addie had been very young, only eight, when her little sister Rebekah died in a tragic accident, whereupon her mother, Rachel, at least in some ways, perished that very same day. Though Rebekah's death had been a terrible shock to Addie too, and her tender heart too had been broken, still she was too young at the time to really understand just how devastating it was for Rachel to lose her. Nor did she or her brother, Wesley, understand why Rachel had always favored Rebekah over them. So, unable to replace her and feeling confused and sad and unloved at home, Addie had found a place of refuge in their neighbor, Claire Ellis. Claire had fostered Addie, nurtured and loved her in a way her own mother couldn't, and despite the difference in their ages, a special bond formed between the two. Over the years, as they were alternately tried and nourished by the necessary despairs and joys of life, their friendship wrought strong—tempered first and foremost by their abiding faith in Christ Jesus the Lord.

Their friendship had remained steady throughout the years. Then, when a terrible fire destroyed Addie's house in Collinsville, forcing her to leave the only home she'd ever known and move to Golden Meadow, she began immediately urging Claire to move and make her home there as well, with her. Initially Claire said no. How could she leave the home she and Luke had shared? She did, however, consent to come there for Christmas, and it was one of the happiest Christmases anyone could remember. Being with Addie, Wesley, and all the children again, the energy and bustle of the holidays – it did perk her up, made her feel better and younger; yet still, she had not been able to make up her mind whether to move or to stay put. In the end it was, to everyone's surprise, Stell Roberts, Wesley's mother-in-law—Laura and Asher's surrogate mother—who put the cap on Claire's decision to move, a decision that turned out to be a happy one for everybody. Bringing only those things she cherished, Claire left the remainder of her possessions behind in Collinsville, giving her house and land to a poor Negro man named Ap Carver. Ap had worked for Claire off and on for years as a handyman, though Claire often joked that he talked ten times more than he worked.

Now as she stood gazing, Addie said her name aloud, "Claire—*in French, the name meant 'clear and bright', a name given to nuns and saints*—my beloved Claire, I remember it all so very well." Raising her cup to her lips, Addie found that the coffee had grown cold.

Turning suddenly, she returned to the kitchen and set the cup in the sink. A minute later, though there were plenty of things needing to be done there at home, she went out the back door and set off at a brisk pace. Walking through the orchard and rounding the gatepost at the gap, she took the back way, cutting through the cornfield, toward Stell and Claire's old house.

The cornstalks were dry, their leaves curled and crisp as paper. As she hurried along, Addie startled a fat field mouse as it sat gnawing kernels from a dried ear of corn, sending the creature skittering for cover under the foliage of a bull thistle. The unexpectedness of it drew her. She stopped and bent over and, for a moment, watched in amusement as the mouse poked its head in and out, stealing jittery peeks at her, its little eyes blinking nervously. The simple encounter lifted Addie's mood, causing her to smile. Straightening up, she closed her eyes and took in a deep breath. The air smelt fresh and good. The smell put her in mind of new hay and cane syrup, apple butter, and boiled peanuts.

Opening her eyes again, she looked around. Before, having been so preoccupied with her own thoughts, she hadn't really taken notice, but now as she stood still and gazed about at her surroundings, she saw and recognized the beauty and fineness in the ordinary things all around her. She thought, *Indeed, this is the day that the Lord hath made.*

The sun was high, the day bright and unclouded. Sunflowers and goldenrod bloomed along the fence and among rows of pumpkins and late squash; cypress vine had claimed most of the fence posts. Bees bumbled in and out of flower heads, and paired with the gentle sway of the flowers in the light breeze, the buzzing sound was near hypnotic. Adding to the ambiance, the cornstalks rustled softly as the lazy current of the day wove through them, and from high in the great, white oak on the far slope of the field, a territorial band of crows grew ever more hysterical over her presence. *Ah, the art and comedy of life,* Addie mused. Eyes and ears charmed anew, she proceeded at a more leisurely pace, stopping once along the way to pick up an arrowhead, turned up by a plow back during the planting season.

When she reached the house, she went up the sagging steps and entered through the unlocked door. The house seemed inhabited by stillness. The front parlor was dim; the curtains were almost completely drawn and what little light there was came in through a small window near the fireplace. Of course, Addie needed none, for she knew every board and cranny of the house; she could see her way through it blind. Noting Stell's chair drawn up to the hearth, she thought, *Stell spent many a winter day rocking in that chair, wrapped up in that old, heavy wool shawl of hers.* The old shawl was still right where Stell left it, hanging on a peg near the fireplace. On the dining table, there was even an old knife, its blade tarnished, and nicked from years of hard use.

Addie saw Claire and Stell all around her. Everything there, all their possessions, from the largest piece of furniture down to the dipper they'd drunk from, had been left mainly untouched for the past three and a half years. All of which now had a story.

Having cherished Claire so, for the longest time after her death, Addie had thought it impossible to ever set foot in this place again, expecting to feel only loss and sorrow. However, once she called together the courage to do so, God, in His steadfast love, met her there, and, instead of feeling sorrowful, she found that being there only brought to mind endearing and happy times, cheered her actually. Over time, it had come to be one of the most peaceful places Addie had ever known.

Presently, she chuckled. *Those two wouldn't do!* Opinionated and outspoken first to last, Stell—as though her very salvation depended on it—had gloried in finding fault with most everyone and everything around her. She took special satisfaction in taking stabs at Claire with her piddling remarks and judgments. Claire, however, armed with a sweet, old-lady smile and a tart wit, relished their jousts and seldom—if ever—let Stell best her.

Thinking this, Addie was smiling as she went down the hall to Claire's room. Going to the window, she pushed the curtain back. Dust flew. The golden light of afternoon streamed in, illuminating the floating motes in the air. A film of dust coated the bedstead and bureau, the writing desk and the chiffonnier. It would have seemed perfectly natural to Addie to have heard Claire say, "Write your name in it if you've a mind to, but date it an' I'll dust your tail feathers!"

On impulse, Addie straightened the spread on the bed and rearranged the pillows. Then, drawn by the smell of old books, she went over to a tier of shelves, neatly lined with volumes of literature and history mostly, some poetry, and a jumble of crumbling periodicals. Idly running her fingers along the middle row, she made a random selection—a leather-bound book with no title. Then without thinking, she flipped it open and began reading. As her eyes traveled slowly over the page, her heart began to pound:

February 10, 1862

A cold, solemn, dreadful day—one I prayed would not come but feared would. A heavy cloud hangs over the South and especially over me. Ten months ago, the very thing they all predicted would happen did happen. Lincoln is a determined cuss, I grant him that. He wouldn't rest until he got his war.

This morning at the break of dawn, my beloved Luke took up arms—said he had to go—as I knew all along he would. Such a surreal scene it was—the gallant parade, the church bell tolling, strains of Dixie floating in the air. He and all the troops were ever so excited. As they stood in formation in front of the post office, they were verily chomping at the bits, so ready to march out, so full of zeal and patriotism—bound for glory! I, however, cannot say I feel the same. My loyalties are divided between two loves.

Before we bid our final farewell, Luke gathered me a small bunch of daffodils. I was still holding them in my hand as I stood watching the procession—the exodus—as it came down Monroe Road. I did manage to wave my handkerchief at him as he marched past, but as soon as I saw his back, I used it to wipe my eyes. Though I held my deepest sorrow from him, my heart was—is—surely breaking. Now the blossoms are pressed within the pages of my Bible. I've no doubt that only my faith and trust in the Lord Jesus Christ will carry me through the long and lonesome days ahead. That my dear husband will come safely back home, back to me, will be a constant prayer on my breath until he and I are reunited.

Addie closed the book and pressed it against her heart. How on earth had she missed this before? A journal! *Claire's* journal! In her mortal hands, she was holding some of her oldest and dearest friend's innermost thoughts and feelings—committed to paper and preserved in Claire's own words! In Addie's mind, she had uncovered a veritable treasure trove.

While she yearned so badly to sit down and continue reading, she knew she'd have to wait. The day was wearing on, and by now Laura would be ready for her to come for Nora. Hugging the journal close, she left the house and started down the lane toward her brother's house, feeling as happy as a little girl on Christmas morning.

CHAPTER 2

He that begetteth a wise child shall have joy of him…and she that bare thee shall rejoice.

—Proverbs 23:24, 25 (KJV)

From the time she was ten years old, the desire of Emily Coulter's heart was to someday become a teacher. Plain and simple, it was her calling. As an invaluable, yet *unpaid*, teacher assistant to Miss Bernice Crowley, she had all but taken over teaching the beginner pupils, insomuch as the position allowed, which meant she was primarily a grammarian. But that wasn't enough for Emily. She knew in order to realize her goal, she must further her education. And so, it was her dream, come next year, to go off to Mississippi Woman's College in Hattiesburg to earn a certificate that would allow her to teach a variety of subjects on different levels. Respectful of the fact that it had been a year of financial disquietude for most folks—crops had failed the year before, and money was scarce—Emily remained prayerful and optimistic, having faith in God and believing with all her heart that He would somehow provide for her college tuition. *Someday,* she would tell herself, *someday.*

That afternoon when school let out, Emily had seen her young niece and nephew, her cousin Meggie, and her little brother home and presently was setting about in preparation to go see a young girl named Belle Robertson, whose family lived about a mile away, at the end of a little road just past the creek bridge.

In the kitchen, Addie was wrapping up a batch of brownies still warm from the oven. "Don't let Belle spoil her supper with these," she said.

"Yes, ma'am." Emily had taken from the back porch a small basket, into which she gently placed a mewling, cocoa-colored kitten. Then, scooping up the plate of brownies, she said, "Bye, Mama, I won't be late."

"Don't you want to eat something before you go?" Addie asked.

"No, ma'am," Emily called over her shoulder as she hurried towards the door. "I don't have time. I'll eat when I get home. See ya!"

"Bye!"

Mabel Claire Robertson, nicknamed Belle, was seven years old, and a student of Emily's, sort of. That spring, along the middle of May, Belle had been thrown from the pony she was riding when the animal became spooked by a snake and reared. Belle suffered a broken back from the accident, and the injury had left both her legs paralyzed. Her parents had been told gravely that she most likely would never walk again and that she would probably be an invalid the rest of her life. Belle's mother had not yet accepted the harsh truth and still prayed for a miracle, but Belle had, and Emily had never seen her sulk in self-pity.

In the beginning, when Belle was convalescing as a bed patient, Emily made a habit of visiting the girl a couple of times a week, primarily to offer her encouragement and bring tidings from Belle's classmates at school. Emily would sometimes pick her flowers, and she would read aloud to her to keep her spirits up. Belle was a bright child who took an interest in learning, so as soon as she was able to sit up again, Emily started giving her lessons and assignments to work on between her visits. Belle loved to star-gaze, and during the summer when the nights were mild, Emily would sometimes go there after dark and point out the various constellations to her. A couple of times, she borrowed a telescope from Miss Bernice so Belle could view the universe more closely, knowing this would delight her. As Belle gazed at the magnified images, Emily had heard her catch her breath in wonder. Gratified, she thought of the third and fourth verses of Psalm 8, where it says, "When I consider thy heavens, the work of thy fingers, the moon, and the stars which thou hast ordained... what is man?"

Belle was a dainty child and sweet-tempered. She had thick, chestnut-brown hair that hung well below her shoulders, which she liked for Emily to brush and plait for her; therefore, Emily would oftentimes take pains weaving and lacing her shiny tresses into intricate braids, sometimes weaving in the flowers she brought. Thus engaged, Belle would sit in joyful anticipation, waiting for Emily to give her a hand mirror so she could inspect her handiwork.

Over time, Emily grew very fond of Belle, and Belle, likewise, had a particularly strong attachment to Emily.

Emily arrived at the house to find Belle sitting in her wheelchair on the porch, a throw across her lap. When she saw Emily, she smiled and asked, "What have you got there?"

"You mean in this basket?' Emily said, teasing her. In that moment, Belle's mother, Julie, stepped out of the house to greet her. Emily addressed her, saying, "Good afternoon, Mrs. Robertson." Extending the covered plate towards her, she added, "Mama sent these brownies for y'all to have with your supper." Of course, Julie was young, only in her twenties, not all that much older than Emily.

Julie took the plate from her gratefully and said, "Your mama's such a thoughtful person, bless her heart. You be sure to tell her I said howdy and thank her for me."

"Yes, ma'am, I will," Emily replied. She went over to Belle and let her look down into the basket.

Belle's smile grew. "What are you doin' with that kitten?" she asked, her big, brown eyes studying her friend-teacher's face.

"I brought her to you, silly, if you want her, an' if your mama says it's all right." But she had already asked Julie, and she had given her consent. She reached for the kitten and handed it to Belle.

"Oh, can I keep her, Mama? She's so soft."

"I don't see why not," Julie replied. "She is a cute little thing."

"Her mama's name is Catherine," Emily said. "I named her after Catherine in *Wuthering Heights*." It was one of Emily's favorite books.

"Do you know what you're going to name her yet?" Julie asked Belle.

Belle thought for a moment. "Well, it's October, and I thought about naming her 'Toby,' but that's a boy's name." She frowned in concentration. Then smiling, she announced, talking mainly to the kitten, "Emily brought us some brownies, and you're brown like chocolate, and really sweet, so I'm gonna call you Brownie."

Though it was late, when everyone else had gone to bed, Addie took Claire's journal from the cedar chest in the parlor and curled up in a chair near the fireplace. The light from the lamp was poor for reading, but she had not been able to get the journal off her mind since finding it that afternoon. She opened it and began reading, starting over with the very first line. When she got to where Claire wrote, "My heart was—is—surely breaking," her eyes misted over, just imagining how alone Claire must have felt and how afraid she must have been—for Luke especially, but for herself as well. A few pages later, she came to read:

September 5, 1862

Me and Rachel—especially Rachel—had us one long day yesterday. We'd been a lot better off if Ol' Doc Barney had stayed out of the way. He proved more of a hindrance than a help, useless as paper scrip. I 'spect that's the very reason he's here instead of off fighting—ever man gone except them too young, too old, or too off in the head to be trusted with a muzzle loader, and Doc qualifies for two of them three, exempting "young." For nigh twenty hours straight, he set with his big belly at the kitchen table, swilling buttermilk and eating ever'thing he could get his hands on. Gobbled up a whole pecan pie before finally passing out cold as a corpse. Messed up ever' dish in the house. I am verily put out with the man—have just in the last hour managed to run the trifling, old sinner back off toward town.

Well, enough of that.

While it was an ordeal, it being her first and all—certainly not an easy or quick birth—Rachel is doing fine, and she has a fine baby boy. He has a head full of dark hair. We didn't have a scale to weigh him on, but I say he'd bring a good eight and a half to 9 pounds. She's calling him Wesley.

I'm plumb wore out and starving to death, haven't slept or eat in two days and cannot write another line.

Addie couldn't help but smile about what Claire wrote about Ol' Doc Barney. Claire always did have a funny way of expressing herself, and for a moment it was almost like she had come back to life and was standing right there in the room with her, going on about it all in person. On the other hand, Addie thought how sad it must have been for Rachel, giving birth to her first child with her husband off fighting in the war, his fate unknown. And how unfair for Samuel too. The whole situation seemed depressing as she thought about all the women who had lived one day to the next just waiting to hear if their loved ones were alive or dead. *That in itself would have been a formidable enemy to fight,* she thought.

Addie marked the page with a satin ribbon and closed the journal. Looking at it and feeling its weight, she judged it to be a hundred pages or better. The way she read, she knew it would take a good while for her to read the whole thing, but she was is no hurry. She had found a way to again spend time with Claire, and she intended to take her time and savor every moment.

She rose from her chair and stretched. When she had put the journal back in the chest, she extinguished the lamp and went down the hall to call it a day.

CHAPTER 3

Yea, the sparrow hath found a home, and the swallow a nest for herself where she may lay her young.

—*Psalms 84:3 (*KJV*)*

"*E*llis Quinn! I *know* you didn't jus' bust a egg on da side o' dis house! How many times I got to say...." The air was chill, the foggy veil of dawn just rising.

Still in her nightgown, with her baby on her hip, Sassie Boone-Quinn stood on the porch watching as her three-year-old son lit out like a bolt of lightning and hid from her behind the henhouse. He was barefoot and had on nothing but a pair of faded overalls. The shiny, black skin, the high cheekbones, the broad nose, and nappy hair—he was his father's son, which filled Obie's heart with more pride than he ever dreamed possible. Thought to be the cutest little boy in the world, Ellis was all rough and tumble, and everyone spoiled him—especially his Pawpaw Ezra and the women at the Preacher's House, the restaurant where Sassie still worked part-time as a cook.

"You best run an' hide 'cauze when I git a-holt o' you wif dis peach limb in my hand, I gone wear you out! You sho gone know what I mean when I says, 'Don't be bustin' no mo' eggs on da side o' dis house'!" Her voice echoed all the way down the packed, clay street.

A time or two, Ellis peeked around the corner tentatively, sneaking glances at his mama, trying to measure the weight of her words. Was she really as mad as she made out like? No. Was she really going to beat the tar out of him with that switch? Probably not. Was there any reason for him to be jealous of his baby sister? Not one. Named after Sassie's sainted "other mother" – the late Claire Ellis – Ellis knew he was his mama's favorite. In her eyes, there was only him. He was her everything.

The third time he stuck his head out, Ellis stepped out of hiding and gave Sassie a sort of shamefaced grin, one she'd seen plenty times before. Having all the advantage he needed, yet understanding fully what was expected of him, he said, "I sorry, Mama."

Trying her best to look and sound stern, Sassie shook the switch at him. "Now. You gone quit all dis showin' out an' do like you tole an' behave yo'self?"

Ellis bowed his head and said, "Yas'm."

Obie and Sassie's café au lait–colored baby girl, Star, had the sunniest disposition imaginable. Her curly hair tangled from sleep, she clutched the yoke of Sassie's gown in her pudgy little fist, as if hanging on for dear life. Unfazed by her mama's scolding tone, she stared up at Sassie's face trustingly and adoringly, her huge, liquid-brown eyes shining with the contentment of just being in her mama's arms and with the assurance of knowing—even in infancy—that she was her favorite. And she was. In Sassie's eyes, Star was the only one. Star was her everything.

Inside the house at the breakfast table, Obie silently ate his biscuits and cane syrup, trying not to think about what everybody else in the quarter was probably thinking—being roused by such calamity right at sunup. Shaking his head, he figured—or rather hoped—that the neighbors might have grown used to his wife's hollering and loud carryings-on by now, as he had. It was just her way. Sassie was good-hearted, fun-loving, and silly—but *loud*. And he could only love her.

Sassie slammed the screen door and returned inside to the kitchen. "Obie, you gone haf to take Ellis wif you today…dat boy done gone slap wild! I caint do a thang wif him! Already dis mawnin' he done—proud as you please—peed on my ferns *an'* busted a egg on da side o' da house!" She playfully rubbed noses with Star and crooned musically, "Yo' daddy done ruint yo' bruther, yes, he has." The baby squealed, delighting in the attention. Turning back to Obie, she said, "An' I still haf to bake dis li'l baby doll's birthday cake an' make us a special supper fo' tonight." She jounced Star in her arms and cooed, "Yes, I do—'cauze it a special day—yes, it iz!"

Obie set his coffee cup down. "Girl, Star ain't nuthin' but a year old. She don't know dis day from all da rest."

"She do too," Sassie corrected him. "Anyway, *I* know an' *you* know."

Star looked at them both and smiled, showing four teeth and two dimples.

Sighing, Obie grabbed his hat and went to them, giving both a kiss on the forehead. "All right den. I reckon Ellis iz goin' wif me." Sassie lifted and waved one of Star's hands at him.

At eighteen, Sassie had never been as happy in her life, except maybe in her early years when her mother was still living. Creenie Boone had been a simple, honest woman with a warm, bright spirit. She and Sassie were very close. In truth, all they had was each other. Sassie was hardly more than a child, only twelve, when Creenie died, and losing her mother had been traumatic and difficult for her. It was as though the lamp in her heart had been extinguished. She was alone, with no family, and filled with despair. Orphaned and uprooted, for the first three years after her mother's death, she had lived with Claire and Stell. And Sassie had loved both of the old ladies dearly, and she dearly loved Addie. And, she knew they all loved her. Yet still, somewhere deep in her soul was a prevailing emptiness, an abiding sense of not belonging that made her feel as though she were completely alone in the world. For the longest time, she had thought she might never find that place she so desperately longed for with all her heart. There were times she felt nothing could fill the emptiness inside her. Then when she was fifteen, she met Obie. To Sassie's thinking, in him, God had given her a gift far more precious than rubies. He was the hope of her heart; she fell head-over-heels in love with him, and gave all of herself to him—heart and body. Obie was, to her, that special place. He was *home*. With him, she belonged.

Equally smitten, Obie had taken Sassie home to meet his family—despite knowing his mother's mind concerning certain things. As he anticipated, Rosette had made a pounce on her, because Sassie was, in her eyes, white. Although it was understandable that she would think so—since there was this: Sassie was a child of rape, the illegitimate bastard of Alfred Coulter, a white man. However, aside from having white blood from her father, and the fact she could easily pass as white, Sassie counted herself to be a Negro, as did everyone else in Dixie. (Hence the old joke that one drop of black blood made one so). Rosette, however, didn't find anything humorous about it.

Then, to top it all off, Sassie became pregnant, sealing any hope of ever being accepted by Rosette. Oh, the disgrace of having a baby on the wrong side of the bed! Oh, was ever someone who called themselves a Christian so unkind! Having no real relatives of her own, Sassie would always remember how much that hurt. But Sassie Boone was not one to faint in the face of adversity. The wedding took place in August that year, and everyone except Rosette was pleased with the union. Obie and Sassie's love was strong. In each other, they found something beautiful and sure.

Feeling a love for him sweeter than honey, Obie's hand was already pushing on the screen door when Sassie called out to him, saying, "Obie Quinn, I hope you know dat youz my very fav'rite."

For in her eyes, there was only him. He was the only one, her everything.

CHAPTER 4

If the Son therefore shall make you free, ye shall be free indeed.

—*John 8:36 (*KJV*)*

November 30, 1862

This morning they found a Negro man lying dead out in front of the mercantile. From all appearances, he most likely either starved or froze to death. He had no papers on him; he died anonymous and was buried in an unmarked grave in Eminence Cemetery. With each passing day we see more and more like him, runaways passing through, experiencing their first taste of freedom, fleeing the security and protection of the only homes they've ever known, with no money, few possessions, and without any plan in mind. It's sad to see them so – lost – confused – scared – not a penny to their name. Times are hard enough for those of us with roofs over our heads.

Last week the weather came right; it turned off cold and held, and though it took some doing, I convinced Rachel into us killing a hog. She didn't think we could do it, just me and her, and I'll admit I myself did wonder, but with the menfolk gone off warring, what choice did we have if we're to make it through the winter?

What a sight we made, covered in blood from head to toe! We'd scalded the hog and had just set to work on scraping it when a black man eased out of the woods and started toward us. Eyes darting all around, he had a look about him such-like I ain't ever seen in a man before. Like some cornered-up, wild animal, he looked both terrified and terrifying.

Rachel was panic-stricken. Knowing her to be weaker than me (in every way), as he came closer I contemplated whether or not I could kill him with a swing of the ax, if need be. It didn't take me a minute to decide I could.

Thank the Good Lord above, it didn't come to that.

There was a movement at the edge of the woods, and a woman and four young'uns showed theirselves. With God as my witness, I can honestly say I had never seen a more pitiful sight in all my born days. They ever one was purely starving, their clothes tattered, nothing but filthy rags— way too thin for the cold we've been having. I hollered and asked the man what he wanted. I did my best to sound brave, though I didn't feel it. Much to our surprise, he said he wanted to help us butcher the hog—in exchange for a meal for his family. He said they had not had any food for several days, that they'd been living mostly on leaves and acorns.

We were glad enough to let him. Me and Rachel stopped what we were doing and cooked all the eggs we could gather up and made a double batch of biscuits. I bade them to come inside and warm by the fire, but they stayed out on the porch, waiting on the food. When it was ready, they attacked it like a pack of ravenous dogs, barely taking time to chew. It's a wonder they didn't all choke to death. So hungry they were, the young'uns forewent using a spoon and just took turns dipping into the berry jam and fig preserves with their fingers. I was afraid they were going to make theirselves sick eating so much, so fast.

While we dressed out the hog, the young'uns bundled up in a quilt and napped in the sun. The woman was watchful as a hawk, wouldn't let them out of her sight for a minute.

Come evening, we all sat down together and feasted on fresh tenderloin, rice and gravy, and cracklin' bread. Nothing in this world compares to the smell of fresh pork sizzling in a pan! As we ate, I couldn't help it—tears sprang to my eyes as I thought about Luke and wondered if he'd had enough to eat that day, wherever he may be. I have not heard a word from him now in over three months and am worried sick. News is slow to come, but we heard that New Orleans fell to the Union back in May, and talk is we lost the Battle of Corinth last month.

We fried up an extra batch of fatback and baked a pone of cornbread for them to pack in the man's haversack for their journey. They didn't talk much, but from what I gathered, they'd made it this far from some'ers 'round Mobile. As to where they aimed to go, the man said, "Some place way to da Nawth, 'cross da mighty river."

Around dark-thirty or so, they all bedded down in the hay. Rachel stayed the night with me—too afraid to go home alone, too afraid to leave me alone, them on the place. Neither one of us slept a wink. When I went out to the barn the next morning, the whole lot of them had disappeared, just left without saying a word. You know how people are sometimes. They took a string of dried apples, but all the quilts were folded and stacked in a neat pile. Other than that, there was no sign of them having ever been here at all.

I 'spect nothing short of a miracle will see them through to their destination—that "some place way to the North" as the man put it. I'm afraid the earthly paradise of milk and honey he spoke of exists only in the poor, misguided hopes and dreams of his race.

The man said his name was Isaac. I heard him call the woman Teena.

Rachel's little Wesley is pleasing in every way; he sleeps most of the time.

Addie closed the journal. She wrapped her arms around herself and stared into the embers of the dying fire, thinking about Claire and Rachel and what all they must have seen and gone through during the war, the loneliness they endured, the hardship. And yet they never let on, never once had they talked about it. She couldn't help but wonder what became of that family. Those four hungry children, had they survived?

With a sigh, she rose and put the journal away. Pondering these things, she started down the long hallway toward her room, seeking the warmth and comfort of her bed, naming her blessings as she went.

CHAPTER 5

But Jesus said, Suffer little children, and forbid them not to come unto me: for of such is the kingdom of heaven.

—Matthew 19:14 (KJV)

*D*uring the first week of November, rain fell steadily for two days, then the skies cleared abruptly, and it turned off bitter cold, the temperature dropping so fast that the ground froze. The mud on the roads became slurry; ice formed in puddles and glazed the water in ditches.

Emily's breath smoked in the biting air. She was wearing a heavy coat, but her hands were cold. She was rubbing them together trying to generate some warmth when Julie Robertson answered the door. Her first words to Emily were, "Belle is awful sick." While Emily stood by the fire warming, she explained how Belle had come down with a bad stomachache Sunday night. That was two days ago. Since then, Belle had not been able to keep food down, and for the last twenty-four hours, she had refused even water. Now, she was running a high fever. The doctor had come and administered his usual remedies for fever and vomiting, but so far, Belle showed little improvement. "He's supposed to come by again this evenin'." She looked anxious, troubled as she said it.

"Can I go in and see her?" Emily asked. "If she's sleeping, I promise not to wake her."

Julie nodded and led the way to Belle's room. Belle's father, Matt, was sitting in a chair at the bedside, wearing a tired, worried look.

Belle's hand was hot when Emily reached and held it. Her face was deathly pale.

She opened her eyes, and Julie bent down and kissed her. "Belle, honey, drink some water," she said. And Belle took a few spoonfuls. Her mama went over to the hearth and got some heated stones and put them under the covers to keep Belle's feet warm, taking the ones that had grown cold back to the fireplace to reheat.

"Will you stay with me, Emily?" Belle asked weakly.

"Yes," Emily said. "Go back to sleep, and I'll be here when you wake up."

That seemed to satisfy her. Belle smiled a little and closed her eyes.

Belle's condition worsened. Thursday morning, the doctor finally said the dreaded word. *Pneumonia.* Belle had pneumonia. Emily wouldn't leave, so Addie stayed with her at the Robertson's house. She kept a fire going in the kitchen stove and kept fresh coffee made. Word spread about how low Belle was, and people came and went, food arrived, prayers were given. Daniel and Amelia came and sat with Matt and Julie for a while, offering whatever encouragement they could.

As Emily sat holding Belle's hand, in a feeble voice, the girl said, "I dreamed about stars, Emily...I dreamed there was a path, and it was all sparkly...a path made out of stars, but when

I stepped on it, it felt like cool grass. I think it was the path to Heaven."

It was in that moment that Emily realized. No one had said so, but she knew. But – Belle was so young, only seven, and she was so pretty, so smart. She had such pretty hair, and she was so bright and so sweet—such a bright, sweet, innocent person. Hadn't she been through enough already? Emily's gaze went to the corner of the room where Belle's wheelchair sat empty. Life was so unpredictable, so uncertain, it seemed so unfair. *Please, God,* she prayed, *don't let this happen.* But she knew that God would take care of Belle. He always had. And Belle would be able to run again, she told herself. She wouldn't need a wheelchair where she was going. *Where she's going, she'll run through streets of gold, and pick flowers from a beautiful garden.* Soon, Belle would be dancing among the stars…*and angels will braid her hair.* When she looked back at Belle, Emily's mind was numb. It was the saddest moment she'd ever known, but she couldn't really feel it.

Belle looked around the room at everyone, her eyes settling on her mother's face. She smiled at her wanly, almost apologetic. Silently, everyone left the room except her parents and the doctor. Soon after, Belle's chest developed an eerie rattle, her breathing became wheezy, and she drifted into a realm of unresponsiveness.

There was a time in the early hours of Friday morning when Addie and Julie sat alone together at the kitchen table. "Emily's been Belle's angel," Julie said. One candle burned on the table. "I won't ever forget how good she's been to her."

Addie acknowledged the words with a smile and gave Julie's hand a gentle squeeze. She had nothing to say; there were no words. Her thoughts shifted then as she remembered how Emily had ministered to her Granny Rachel after she had a stroke. Not much older than Belle at the time, every night Emily would groom Rachel's hair; she had brought her little gifts—a cool rock, a bird's nest, kittens, flowers—and laid them in her hands. With tears in her eyes, she said, "Emily has a good heart. She's a good girl and a good daughter." *A blessing...*

Julie got up and went to the window and looked out. In a sort of numb-mindedness, she said, "Looks like another frosty mornin'." The young mother's eyes were glazed with fatigue. She was exhausted, understandably. She had tended to Belle for months, ever since the accident, nursed her so lovingly. She'd done everything she could possibly do to make Belle's life seem normal. And now, there was nothing she could do that would make a difference. She just stood there, staring off into space, grappling with the thought that Belle might leave and never return.

Her thoughts were cut short when Matt stepped out of Belle's room, a ravaged look on his face, and motioned for his wife. Suddenly the couple was clinging to each other in panic and grief, realizing they were about to go in and say farewell to their only child. It was too soon, too hard, too overwhelming. Too unbearable. A few, short minutes later, a long, agonizing wail of pain permeated every board in the house. "No, no, no, Belle, oh, please, no." Hearing this, everyone knew that Belle's little soul had been lifted up into Heaven, and that Matt and Julie's world had ended.

Throughout the house, women held and consoled one another, weeping. Emily sobbed uncontrollably as Addie held her. "I'm sorry," Addie whispered. "I know you loved Belle. I know she was very special to you."

Emily pulled away from her finally. Unable to stop crying, she reached for her coat and managed only to say, "I'm walking home."

The rest of the day was long and bleak, despite the dazzling sunshine. Emily lay face-down on her bed with her arms over her head, crying for what seemed like hours, finally crying herself to sleep. Later, Addie went in to her and sat down on the bed beside her. Touching her arm reassuringly, she said, "You were a good friend to Belle; she loved you very much. Y'all were lucky to have each other."

Through a wave of fresh tears, Emily replied, in the merest whisper, "I was the lucky one."

Addie sat there quietly for a few minutes more and stood up. She knew there were no words she could say to make it all right, nothing that would change anything, or help anything, so she didn't try. Given time, she knew it wouldn't hurt as bad. In time, Emily's heart would mend. Tears rolled down Addie's face as she thought of Belle's parents. How well she knew the pain they were feeling, for she too had lost a child. But all she could do was pray for God to draw nigh to them and comfort them and give them peace. Right then, in the silence of her heart, she said a prayer for them, and for Emily.

She bent down and kissed Emily's silky hair and said softly, "Night-night, I love you."

The next day, the day of Belle's funeral, Addie knocked softly on Emily's bedroom door and entered. Emily was sitting on her bed, deep in concentration, with paper and a pencil. She seemed to be calm, not crying anymore.

"You all right?" Addie asked.

Without raising her eyes from her writing, Emily nodded and said, "I'm better. I'm fine."

"Well, it's about time to go."

"All right, Mama, just give me a few more minutes."

Standing behind the pulpit, Brother Higgins looked out at the congregation and began solemnly, "We gather here today, dear friends, with sorrowful hearts, to say good-bye to our little sister in Christ, Mabel Claire Robertson."

The service was heart wrenching and brief; the church was full. Brother Higgins talked about Belle's strength and courage, about what an inspiring and sweet child she was, and about how much she was loved. He referenced Scripture that identified children as a heritage of the Lord, a gift, a blessing, and he read from the book of Matthew, about how Jesus called the little children unto Him and His instructions thereafter to the disciples concerning children. He spoke of eternal life through Christ the Lord.

Matt and Julie clutched each other through the entire eulogy and sermon, weeping uncontrollably. There was not a dry eye in the church.

Afterward, when they went to the cemetery for the interment, Brother Higgins imparted that Emily had something she wanted to read as a tribute to Belle, as her friend. Far from being plain, Emily looked, and was, so much like her mother. She had intelligent, blue eyes and a keenly observant, confident air about her. She was wearing a dark-blue dress and looked somber and respectful as she stepped close to the freshly dug grave. In a strong voice, she started reading:

MABEL CLAIRE

Along the green lane in the Maytime,
I gathered the violets blue,
Echoing yet with the beesong,
And the cool of the morning dew.
Gathered them for sweet Mabel,
Beautiful Mabel Claire,
To clasp in her dainty fingers,
To braid in her shining hair.

Again when the summer was finest,
For the love of her brown, brown eyes,
I gathered her royal roses,
As bright as the sunset skies.
Gathered them for sweet Mabel,

Beautiful Mabel Claire,
To clasp in her dainty fingers,
To braid in her shining hair.

But now comes the dreary November,
Making me to mourn and weep,
For folding her dainty fingers,
Mabel has gone to sleep.
Closing her brown eyes gently,
Beautiful Mabel Claire,
No more shall I gather the roses
To braid in her shining hair.

As Emily read, tears rolled down her face unattended. The poem was a testimony of hers and Belle's friendship, and a heartfelt expression of her feelings. Writing the words brought about a sort of healing, and reading them aloud gave her a sense of closure. When she was finished, Brother Higgins said a final prayer and led the congregation in a closing hymn:

Oh, they tell me of a home far beyond the skies,
Oh, they tell me of a home far away;
Oh, they tell me of a home where no storm clouds rise,
Oh, they tell me of an unclouded day.

CHAPTER 6

And God shall wipe away all tears from their eyes; and there shall be no more death, neither sorrow, nor crying...

—*Revelation 21:4 (*KJV*)*

One day gave way to the next, and it was sunny and cold Saturday morning when Hiram and Addie went to town. After Hiram drew up and stopped the wagon, he set off in the direction of the post office while Addie proceeded across the street to the general store, with her shopping basket and list.

The bell over the door tinkled as she entered. Inside, her nose met with the sweetness of citrus and the potent aroma of coffee. She and the clerk behind the counter swapped salutations. Two men were pulled up close to the stove playing checkers; another stood, watching them play. Addie took her time and wandered around the store, browsing. It was time to think of Christmas gifts, even though there wouldn't be much money to spend this year.

The store stocked almost any item a person needed that they couldn't grow or make themselves. They carried pots and kettles, utensils, tableware, crocks, and jars. There was a dry-goods section with bolts of material for making clothing, bedsheets, pillowcases, and tablecloths, and a section for sewing notions—threads, needles, pins, scissors, embroidery hoops, thimbles, ribbons, rickracks, and yarns. They sold shoes, socks, and stockings. They stocked medicinal items such as tinctures, liniments, castor oil, salts, and soap. There was a shelf for snuff, chewing tobacco, cigars, and chewing gum. Jars of candy lined the counter. They sold knives and toys, paper, pencils, and ink; and this time of year they had crates of oranges and bushel baskets of lemons and raisins and nuts. The heart of the store shelved food staples—salt, sugar, spices, cornmeal, oatmeal, flour, coffee beans, cocoa, yeast, vinegar, honey, and vanilla. This is the area where Addie was when she heard, "Hey, Aunt Addie. Somethin' I can help you with?"

It was her fourteen-year-old nephew, Jesse—Wesley and Laura's son. Tuesdays and Thursdays after school and all day on Saturday, Jesse worked at the store stocking shelves, making deliveries, carrying bags for customers, and lending a hand to load heavy sacks and barrels onto wagons when needed. Jesse was an earthy, easygoing boy with an infectious grin, and his amiable disposition gained him the affections of almost everyone. He never met a stranger; he waved and spoke to everyone on the street, even the horses, mules, and dogs of the store's regular patrons. Nothing bored him more than school, but he loved working at the store.

"Why, hey, Jesse," Addie greeted him. "I don't really need any help, thank you, but you can keep me company while I shop." Then she remembered and said, "Here, let me take a look at that eye." She reached and tilted his face more toward the light. Shaking her head disapprovingly, she exclaimed, "Oh my, your mama said you had a shiner, and she wasn't lying! Does it hurt?"

"No, ma'am." Jesse looked mildly pleased as his aunt fussed over him.

"Well, that Junior Tucker ought to be ashamed of himself, but I'm proud of you for trying to help Wiley. Emily said if Junior wasn't so much older and bigger than you, he'd been whistling a different tune the other day."

Junior Tucker was a natural-born troublemaker who liked nothing better than to pick on all the other boys at school, particularly those younger than him. For no reason other than meanness, he had tripped Wiley Parker and made him fall. Wiley had gotten up and was in the process of dusting off his pant legs when Junior gave him a hard shove, knocking him to the ground again. Having had a bate, the next time Wiley got up, he rushed Junior and caught a fist to the side of his head. Seeing his friend so outsized, Jesse had leaped on Junior's back. Miss Bernice had come out quickly and broke the fight up, but not before Jesse got slugged in the eye. Even though he had lost the fight, Jesse was in his glory all the same. It was worth it to him just to have gotten a few good licks in.

"I can't stand him," Jesse said, "him or his brother—always struttin' around like they rule the world. I wish they'd both get struck by lightnin'." He had seen Junior's older brother, Talmage, trying to intimidate Sassie a time or two. It seemed to be his idea of a joke to keep her from walking on the boardwalk, evidently just because she was black. And when he was younger, Jesse had been secretly in love with Sassie, or rather he'd had a boyish crush on her, and he felt very protective of her still.

Addie smiled at him. "You wait. Those two will meet their match someday."

When Addie paid her bill, Jesse walked with her to the wagon, with her bag in the crook of his arm. "Hey, Uncle Hiram!" he called.

Hiram had bought a newspaper and was leaned up against the wagon reading it, but when he saw Addie and Jesse approaching, he folded it up. "Howdy," he said. He then pointedly took a minute to make over Jesse's black eye, telling him, "That's a real humdinger you got there." Grinning from ear to ear, Jesse said good-bye to them and headed back across the street toward the store. Hiram helped Addie into the seat and handed her the mail. "Got a letter from Wilkes," he said. Wilkes was Hiram's younger brother, who lived in Virginia on their parents' old homestead.

Immediately, Addie wondered to herself if he was writing to say he was coming for a visit. *Sweet Lord in heaven, I hope not*, she thought. Wilkes had visited once and overstayed his welcome, to say the least. "Mmm," she said. "What did he have to say?" Of course she would read the letter for herself later.

Hiram answered drily, "Not much of anything, said he had a good yield on his tobacco crop…oh, an' that his business partner sold out his share to him an' moved off to California—"

They were interrupted then as Bernice Crowley, the schoolteacher, came bustling down the sidewalk toward them. "Good! I'm so glad I caught y'all before you left!" She was near out of breath. Bernice was a plump, cheerful woman with gray hair and happy eyes and an airy manner. "Forgive me. I don't mean to infringe upon your day"—her bosom was rising and falling—"but I wonder if you might have time to talk to me for a few minutes. We can go to the school where it's quiet." The town had bought the house that once belonged to Travis and Abigail when they moved to Memphis, and it now served as the schoolhouse; it was located just down the street. As Hiram and Addie stared at her curiously, Bernice said, "It concerns Emily."

The week before Thanksgiving, since cold weather had set in, most everyone in the community butchered hogs and, for several days henceforth, glutted on fresh pork. Once again, smokehouses were full, and meat was plentiful.

Matt and Julie Robertson became more withdrawn with every passing day. After Belle's funeral, life had recommenced and went on as usual for everyone else, and after a few days, visits dwindled, and the young couple was left to themselves, to tread sorrow's path alone. Julie slept much of the time, giving little care to how she looked; Matt had started drinking heavily. Whereas before they had been faithful to attend church, since Belle died, they had quit altogether. Concerned about them, on Tuesday evening the week following Thanksgiving, Daniel and Amelia left the children with Hiram and Addie and went to pay them a visit; Amelia had made them a sweet potato pie.

When they walked up on the porch and knocked on the door, they heard no one but waited, figuring that eventually someone would come. There was a profound sense of sadness about the place, as though gloom had settled on the premises. After a few minutes, Julie opened the door. Politely enough, she invited Amelia in. "Matt's somewhere around back," she told Daniel.

Amelia followed Julie into the house. Julie went straight into the parlor and sat down in a rocker by a window and looked out, so listless she might have been asleep with her eyes open. The house was as quiet and cold as a tomb. There was a small fire burning in the fireplace; the kitten Emily had given Belle was curled up on the couch. Amelia set the pie on a table and sat down on the couch beside the kitten. "Today was a pretty day, wasn't it?" she began hopefully.

Julie made no answer.

"We just wanted to come by and see how you and Matt were getting along," Amelia added. Looking around, she ventured, "Have y'all had supper yet?" There was no smell of cooking in the house; Julie had grown noticeably thin, her eyes were sunken, and there were dark circles under them. "Maybe I can help you fix something, or how about I take this pie to the kitchen and make us some coffee?"

Without turning to look at Amelia, Julie said dully, in a sort of bored way, "I'm sure you'll forgive me for not being a better hostess, but I didn't realize this was a social call. How 'bout you just go ahead and bestow whatever advice it is you've come to give me and be done with it. Seems like that's all anyone comes for anyway, to give us advice." She said it more in the way of annoyance than anger. Continuing to stare out the window, she sighed and said, "Let me see. So far, I've been told I should get rid of all of Belle's things; after all, they're just painful reminders." As if she needed anything to remind her of her. "And someone said I should stop visitin' her grave every day, like I'm supposed to just leave her up there, in the cemetery, all alone, forget her. Oh, and let's not forget—Matt and I should get busy and have us another baby as soon as possible." Like that would replace the child they lost, like anything could replace their precious Belle. She didn't bother to say that she and Matt rarely even talked anymore, that he stayed in the barn most of the time, drinking, and that he usually passed out on the couch long before she went to bed every night.

Amelia looked at her quietly, sympathetically. She could only imagine the pain Julie and Matt were feeling. Their loss was devastating, and she knew their lives would never be the same again. But it could someday be better again, if they tried. She wanted to go over and touch Julie, take her hand, or hug her, but she was afraid Julie didn't want her to, that she might think of it as pity, and Amelia didn't want to offend her. She reached over and petted the kitten. Shaking her head, she said, "No. No advice. That's not why I came. I just came to see how you're doin', just to talk, because I care about you."

Tears sprang to Julie's eyes. After a long pause, her voice trembling, she said, "I'm sorry…I know people mean well… but you tell me…how do we get through this? How do we go on?" She could not imagine having to live the rest of her life in such pain, or that she would even live through it. Sometimes she

wished she could just close her eyes and never open them again...
just fade from existence.

Amelia replied to the question as honestly as she could, "Only
by the grace of God, and only one day at a time."

Going across the backyard, Daniel found Matt in the barn
sharpening an ax with a grindstone. Daniel spoke; Matt nodded
in greeting.

"Just came by to see how y'all're doin'," Daniel said. "Amelia's
up in the house talkin' to Julie."

"Doin' the best we can, I reckon. Ain't no use in complainin',"
came the reply.

Matt continued to work. Neither man spoke for a few minutes.
Daniel couldn't help but notice how hollow-eyed and haggard
Matt looked; he actually looked sick. Daniel's eyes rested on an
open bottle of whiskey on the worktable. "Been missin' y'all at
church," he said. "Was hopin' we might see you there this Sunday."

Matt made a little business of testing the ax blade with his
finger then went back to sharpening it. Without looking up, he
replied, "We just takin' it all a day at a time, just tryin' to find some
peace of mind."

Daniel took a deep breath. Though he took pity on Matt
for what he was going through, he said, "Well, you ain't gonna
find none in the bottom of that there bottle, I can tell you that
for sure."

Matt looked up at him steely, his eyes held on Daniel's face like
a pointed gun. He reached for the whiskey and took a deliberate
swig straight from the bottle, to show just how brazen he could
be. "That right?" he said, wiping his mouth on his sleeve.

Daniel didn't cow. "That your plan, Matt? To try an' drown
your sorrows in whiskey?"

Matt cocked his head back. "Your plan to come here an' meddle in my business, try an' tell me how to live?" He said it a little rough, with a little challenge.

Daniel shook his head. "No," he said. "An' I ain't here to judge you neither. Fact is, I'd like to help you."

"Go home," Matt said. "Leave us be."

"No disrespect intended, but I can't do that," Daniel said.

Changing the tack of the conversation, Matt asked, "You ever had to bury a young'un, Daniel?"

Daniel allowed a pause to be his comment, knowing that Matt knew the answer.

Matt said, "Well, I pray you never do."

"Just because I ain't lost a child," Daniel said, "that don't make me a stranger to trouble. My pa—Alfred Coulter—well, there ain't time left in the world to go in to all the particulars– " How did a man go about telling someone that his father had raped and impregnated two women: one of them black, the other his own wife? "Let's just say he had his own brand of meanness, an' until he was finally shot an' killed, he tore up all of creation an' put my family through hell an' half an acre." He pointed at the bottle of whiskey and continued, "Him, an' Amelia's pa, and her ma— they all three was sorry drunkards. So take it from somebody that knows—you don't want to be a sorry drunkard, an' Julie does not want or deserve to have a sorry drunkard for a husband."

Matt's head went down; his eyes grew wet. Once again, he gave in as the grief coursing through his body hit him full force. He cried raspingly, "I miss my little girl, Daniel. I want her back…I want Belle back *now*." But Belle was gone, forever. She was dead. One day the two of them had been laughing and playing with her little kitten; the next week, they had buried her.

In a more benevolent tone, Daniel said, "I know you do; we all do. But as hard as it is to accept, Belle's in a better place now." After a minute, he said, "God's made a way for you to see her again, though. You can spend all of eternity with her, but it's up to you whether or not you do."

Matt wiped his tears. "I know...Julie an' me both have been saved. We believe—"

"Believin' is the first step, an' sadly that's as far as some folks ever get," Daniel said. "But if you keep readin', you'll see that ain't all there is to it. We have to let God be the Lord of our lives; we have to obey Him and keep His commandments, become servants." Daniel stopped himself, taking a few moments to reorder his thoughts. "Look, man, I didn't come here to preach. I can't imagine what you're goin' through, an' I sure didn't mean to upset you more than you already are. I know you're hurtin', an' I hurt for you, and for Julie. It's just that I wasted a lot of precious time lettin' bitterness eat away at my insides, an' I hate to see you let the devil take you down that same dead-end road. Now. I wish you'd pour out the rest of that whiskey an' go up to the house with me an' let's have a cup of coffee an' a piece of that sweet 'tater pie."

Matt stood for a minute, contemplating. Finally, hesitantly, he reached over and screwed the cap back on the bottle. Almost smiling at Daniel, he said, "Well, the pie sounds good."

Daniel nodded. He guessed that was plenty enough for one day. It was at least a start.

CHAPTER 7

Delight thyself also in the Lord: and He shall give thee the desires of thine heart.

*—Psalms 37:4 (*KJV*)*

$\mathcal{B}$ y the middle of December, hardly a day passed that the womenfolk didn't bake something in preparation for Christmas; wonderful smells filled the air. They decorated with pine boughs and holly, and a few days before Christmas, Hiram and Samuel went into the woods and cut a fat cedar, which Hiram brought home over his shoulder and was later decorated by the whole family; Jesse and Wiley Parker shot down a globe of mistletoe, which they used to terrorize all the girls at school, chasing them with it relentlessly.

On Christmas Eve, they all went to church to attend the candlelight service. Lit by a hundred candles and decorated with greenery and white and gold ribbons, inside the church there was a sort of sweet hush... *from angels bending near the earth to touch their harps of gold...* Therein lay a sort of reverent stillness... *to hear the angels sing...* This was holy ground, and as the organist softly played "It Came Upon the Midnight Clear," the Spirit stirred among them, and the presence of the King of kings could be felt.

They stood and sang, "Silent night! Holy night! All is calm, all is bright..." And as the music and words of the first stanza filled the church, the door opened and closed quietly, and Matt and Julie Robertson stepped inside and made their way down the aisle to an empty pew.

On Christmas morning, everyone attended their own, opening presents and breakfasting at their own houses. Then midafternoon, the entire family gathered at Hiram and Addie's for the Christmas feast. There were sixteen in all there for dinner: Hiram and Addie, Emily, Samuel, and Nora; Wesley and Laura, Jesse and Meggie; Daniel and Amelia, Rachel and Carson; Laura's twin brother, Asher, and his second wife, Penelope, and daughter Libby.

The women had worked tirelessly over the meal, and when everything was ready, it was a sight to behold. The table and sideboard were loaded with food. There was succulent baked ham, chicken and dumplings, corn bread dressing, mashed potatoes, butterbeans and peas, turnip greens, deviled eggs, corn bread and rolls, fried apple pies, pecan pie, fruitcake, and divinity candy. In honor of Claire, Addie had made teacakes, and there was a sweet potato casserole, which had been Stell's favorite dish.

Staring at the table hungrily, Jesse swallowed and declared, "I can't wait to dig in!" And after the blessing was said, dig in they did!

Conversation around the table was animated, with several conversations going on at once, all part of the same one. Amelia told of receiving a letter from her Aunt Jennie in Collinsville, how Ap had gotten married some months before, and that his wife was expecting. Oh, wouldn't Claire be tickled pink to know her little house would again be raising a family within its walls? About fifteen minutes into the meal, they were laughing and talking, when there came a knock on the front door. Addie rose from her chair to answer it, saying, "Strange. I wonder who that could be?" She opened the door, and Bernice Crowley was standing there. With a smile of surprise, Addie said, "Why, Merry Christmas! Come in! You're just in time to pull up a chair and have dinner with us!"

Bernice bustled in excitedly. "Glad tidings and Merry Christmas to you all! I didn't mean to interrupt your meal, but when you see what I have to show you, you'll understand why I couldn't wait!" When she saw Laura get up and start making room for her at the table, she said, "I'm too excited to sit down yet!"

As all eyes settled on her, she said, "As you all know…of course, you probably don't know, because I didn't tell anyone." She waved her hand, dismissingly, and went on. "Anyway, the day school let out for Christmas, I traveled to Ellisville to my cousin Charlotte's house for a visit; she is a dear, and I just returned home yesterday. Oh, she has the most beautiful things, and, Hiram, I told her how talented you are at making furniture, and she was so delighted. She's sent you a picture from a magazine of a cabinet she wants you to make for her. I told her you would deliver it right to her door, and I'm to give you her address so you and she can get together on a price and work out all the details. She said there's no hurry about it—"

"I'm obliged," Hiram said. "Me an' Daniel were needin' us a new project."

Bernice went on, "At any rate, that's not the reason I've come." She exclaimed, Oh, dear Lord!" Then she burst into laughter. Everyone stared at her wonderingly, she was acting so strange. She closed her eyes and caught a breath quickly.

"Do you need some water?" Addie asked.

Bernice shook her head no. When she had composed herself, she said, "Forgive me. I'm just giddy with excitement."

They all waited as patiently as they could for her to continue. Confound the woman—would she ever get to the point!

"So, yesterday, when I got back into town, I went to the post office to see if I had any mail." It was then that she reached into her coat pocket and withdrew a letter. "Ta-da!" She went over and held it out to Emily. "Emily dear, I want you to read this."

Emily looked about, confused. She reached and took the letter, hesitantly, and when her eyes met Bernice's, she asked, "What is it?"

Bernice's eyes were shining. She said, "Go on, read it."

Hiram and Addie glanced at each other, a vague smile coming to their faces. Could it be?

Emily read, while the others at the table looked on anxiously. When she came to the end, she looked up at Bernice, a baffled look on her face. "I...I don't understand," she stammered. The contents of the letter were so confusing.

Bernice responded gaily, "It's all right there in the letter. Last month I wrote to the headmistress at the Woman's College and sent her a transcript of all your grades, and I explained how you've been working as my assistant and how you home-schooled Belle"—she looked over at Addie— "and with a little help from your mother, I entered a copy of your poem in a writing contest sponsored by the college, *and you won!* Isn't it wonderful? No doubt the very angels in Heaven weep in our gladness!"

It still wasn't registering in Emily's brain. What did this mean? What had she won? "But—"

Bernice was beside herself. Her eyes were glistening with happy tears. "Congratulations, Emily! You've won yourself a scholarship to go to college!" All of a sudden, there were shouts of joy and a burst of applause from everyone seated around the table; then everyone started talking all at once.

This couldn't be! It was too good to be true! Emily could scarcely breathe. This was the last thing she expected to hear. She looked around in disbelief. "Is this serious, or are y'all just pullin' my leg?"

she asked. Then suddenly, the reality of it, the *thrill* of it, started to sink in. They weren't kidding with her. This was really real. She had long dreamed of this very thing, and now her dream was coming true. Her mind was spinning out of control. The sound she made was one of pure joy as she jumped up and ran over to hug Bernice. Next, she went and hugged her mama, then Hiram, then everyone else, all of them crying and sharing in her happiness. Clapping her hands together, she gushed, "Oh gosh! Oh my goodness! I'm goin' to college! Thank you, thank you, thank you, God! I'm goin' to college!"

It was the best Christmas present ever.

Claire's journal told of an altogether different Christmas:

December 25, 1862

It sure ain't seemed nothing like Christmas today, just another long, dreary, sad day. Me and Rachel cooked us a meal and ate it, but it weren't nothing special.

My heart aches for Luke so, I find it hard to even write. I've thought about him all day (what else?), him out in this wet, cold weather. I pray he has warm-enough clothes on and is somehow managing to stay dry. God, please provide for him, and all our brave men.

A cold, gray rain has fell all day, and falls even still as I write. The angels in Heaven no doubt weep over our dire and dreadful circumstance...

CHAPTER 8

A time to weep, and a time to laugh; a time to mourn, and a time to dance.

*—Ecclesiastes 3:4 (*KJV*)*

On New Year's Day the following week, it was a comparatively smaller group that gathered around the Quinn's kitchen table for dinner. There was only Ezra and Rosette, Georgianne, Obie and Sassie, Ellis and Star. Rosette cooked a pot of black-eyed peas and a pot of cabbage—both seasoned with a hunk of cured hog's head—and rice and corn bread. She opened a quart jar of pickles and sliced an onion; there was a pitcher of sweet tea, and Sassie made two pecan pies, which was Georgianne's favorite. Ellis, who especially loved going to his grandparents' house, looked upon the meal like all the meals he ate there, as a party given in his honor. There, he could have as many pieces of pie as he wanted. He was even allowed his own cup of coffee, just like his pawpaw's, only watered down. While there, he would spend hours in his pawpaw's barn, exploring and busying himself with the fascinating gadgets he discovered. His favorite contraption was one that would shell corn, and as he fed dried ears into the grinder and turned the rusty handle, Ezra would watch him in quiet joy.

It was a day of lassitude, albeit not an unhappy one. The talk around the table, like the victuals, was plain yet sustainable. Everyone ate their fill; no one complained, not even Rosette, perhaps giving credence to the old adage "Enough is a plenty." When dinner was over, as soon as the men and Ellis went outside to walk the grounds, Sassie, preoccupied with her own thoughts, went to the sink and started washing the dishes Rosette had set to soak earlier. Georgianne had begun yawning even before she finished eating, but she got up and joined Sassie in clearing the table. She scraped the plates into the slop bucket and dropped the dirty silverware into a dishpan of hot, soapy water. The remaining rice had grown cold and clumpy; she set it on the stove, along with the leftover peas and cabbage, putting the few remaining slices of corn bread and pecan pie in the pie safe. Sassie took a wet rag and wiped the table. Star sat on Rosette's lap while Rosette sang, "Shoo fly, don't bother me, shoo fly, don't bother me." She clapped Star's hands as she sang the ditty, making the baby laugh. Shortly thereafter, she passed her to Sassie for a diaper change. It was cold, and before long the men drifted back to the house, bringing in an armload of firewood; Obie threw a few more pieces on the fire. Ezra sat and did his best to look attentive to the conversation, but soon dozed off with Ellis on his lap. Star grew restless and started getting into things. Bored out of her mind, Georgianne announced that she was tired and ready to go home. When Sassie began collecting their coats, Obie rose to help her. Rosette protested their leave-taking and said that they might as well just stay for supper, though she would never have forgiven them if they had, and they knew it.

Another family dinner thus concluded.

The hour was late, Obie figured close to midnight, as he lay in the bed staring toward the ceiling. He took a deep breath and let it out. He, they, had put off talking about it as long as they could, and though he'd sooner not talk about it at all, he knew they had to. He coughed and cleared his throat. The time had come, he reckoned. No sense putting it off any longer. Turning to face her, he rose up on one elbow and whispered, "Sassie, you 'wake?"

Beside him, Sassie lay still. She could feel the throbbing in her neck and wrists, knowing what was coming. "I 'wake," she said. She heard Obie take another deep breath.

"Well, you bin thankin' 'bout it, what we talked about?" he whispered nervously.

Sassie didn't say anything for a minute. He'd give her a mess of things to think about. "Some," she said.

"Well? Don't you thank it a good idea?"

No, she thought grudgingly. *Ain't nothin' good about it, far as I can see.* Her throat burned.

Obie could feel her emotions working and could just about guess what she was thinking. He said softly, sounding rehearsed, "Daddy done did a day's work 'fore I ever git out dere ever' mawnin'. He gittin' old now; he need more help, 'specially wif da heavy work, wif da plowin' an' all."

Sassie swallowed the tears in her throat. "It jus'…I ain't never thought about us livin' nowhere else but here." And that's what this was about, them leaving here to go live someplace else. More specifically, it was about them leaving here and going to live with his mama and daddy so he could help Ezra run the farm. The very thought of it filled her with dread. Not that this place was anything fancy, but it had been their home for four years, and they had made it a happy, cheerful home. She wanted them to stay here, in their own house, *this* house.

"Girl, look at all us up in here." Obie gestured toward the foot of the bed, where Ellis and Star were asleep on a pallet, on the floor. "Dis house be bustin' at da seams."

Remembering the itty-bitty two-room cabin in Collinsville where she, her mama, and her Auntie Dorrie had lived, Sassie thought, *Wusn't room to cuss a cat, but da three of us made it jus' fine.* That fact aside, she decided to bring it on home to him. "Obie Quinn, has you even thought 'bout how we gone…*you know*, wif yo' mama an' daddy jus' *right dere?*" What sort of privacy could they hope to have? *Not that it would bother him probably.*

Obie smiled in the dark. "Girl, how you thank we be livin' now? Folks be all round us. Miz Essie stay so close she can look in one side dis house an' see clean out da other. She prob'ly list'nin' to ever' word we sayin' right now." For effect, he called out over his shoulder, "Hey, Miz Essie!" Then, more seriously, twisting a lock of Sassie's hair around his finger, he said, "Anyway, Mama an' Daddy ain't gone be jus' *right dere*; dey be plenty o' room fo' all us. We gone be in our own room, all to ourself. An' Ellis an' Star gone have dey own room. Now won't dat be somethin' to see—dem chilluns sleepin' in dey own bed?"

Dey a world mo' to it than dat! A tear slid from the corner of Sassie's eye as she thought, *An' Miz Essie a far cry from yo' mama!* Even though Obie knew how Rosette was, it was different for him. She was his mama. He'd grown up with her and her ol' ugly ways. *An' God don't like ugly!* She said, "Jus' makes me kinda sad…leavin' ever'body…all our neighbors…Auntie Georgianne." Mr. Ezra was as nice as could be, but she'd never survive under Rosette's rule. Misery, multiplied by a zillion! Just thinking about it made her belly hurt like she'd been eating green plums. *Dis gone be da end of me fo' sho.*

Obie replied, "It ain't like we goin' far, jus' a little ways out of town—an' Auntie Georgianne all time be goin' out to Mama's."

"Exactly," Sassie said sullenly, "to 'Mama's'." *An' who am I?* The whole thing just didn't seem fair.

Not knowing what else to say, Obie dropped back on his pillow with a despairing sigh.

Suddenly, Sassie felt ashamed and sorry. She realized how selfish she was acting, like a child set on having her own way. Obie was a good man, kind and gentle. He'd proved his love for her time and again, had made a promise to God, and to her, to take care of her and never leave her. Deep down, she knew he was just trying his best to make a way for their little family. He had brought the subject up for them to talk about like they had a choice, but she knew they really had no say-so in the matter. Truth be told, the reason they couldn't stay here in this house was because they couldn't afford it. The rent came due on the fifteenth, in two weeks, and they simply didn't have money to pay it. Of course, they were used to not having much money and had learned to make do on what Obie made helping Ezra, and what little she made working at the Preacher's House. Still, it wasn't enough. And whereas she would have gladly taken in some washing and ironing for a few extra dollars, no one around there could afford such a luxury anymore. Times were hard for everyone.

Tears flowed from her eyes. She didn't want to leave here, and the last thing she wanted to do was move in with her in-laws, but she knew they had to. She thought, *for whither thou goest, I will go...thy people shall be my people...* No one said she had to like it, but she knew she must do this, and not begrudgingly—*for richer, for poorer*—but for Obie.

She turned to Obie then and slipped her arm around his waist. She said, "For a fact, dat will be somethin' to see—Ellis an' Star sleepin' in dey own beds. *But* yo' mama needn't be thankin' she fixin' to ham-hack me over ever' li'l thang."

There was a marked silence. She had said it so solemn it took a minute for Obie's mind to grasp what she said. As it came to him, he looked down at her searchingly, and then he began to laugh. She had sounded so serious, which only made it funnier to him, which set him to laughing harder. Trying to keep his voice down so he wouldn't wake the children, he laughed until he was weak, a yoke of worry having been lifted from his mind. Everything was going to be all right. Sassie would see. Happy enough to dance a jig, as he leaned down to kiss her, all he could say was, "A sight, fo' sho! Won't it be?"

It was almost two weeks later, on January 12, 1907, when the move took place. Ezra's wagon was loaded to the hilt. Sassie took everything that belonged to them, right down to the eggs the chickens had laid that morning.

"Yaw ready?" Ezra asked, after Obie handed Star to Sassie and climbed up after them. Ellis was sitting next to his pawpaw, grinning like a minstrel. When Obie gave the go-ahead, Ezra clucked to the mule, and they moved forth slowly.

As the wagon went down the dirt street, several of their old neighbors watched and waved from their yards and porches; some hollered. Sassie willed herself to smile and waved back, but there were tears in her eyes. She knew she was going to miss this place.

She missed it already.

That same afternoon, Emily stood on the wooden platform at the train depot, surrounded by some of those she loved and some of those who loved her. When the whistle blew and the conductor called out "All aboard!" they knew this was farewell. Emily threw her arms around her mother, and for a long moment they held each other, their eyes filled with bittersweet tears. When they let each other go, Emily hugged Hiram one last time before boarding the train.

Steam hissed, pistons churned, iron screeched. As Emily waved at them through the window, just for a moment Addie caught a glimpse of a wide-eyed, pig-tailed little girl. She had always known this day would come but never realized just how quickly. But she was at peace with it. She knew Emily would be fine. When the train started moving, she moved with it along the platform for a few steps, smiling and waving. Filled with a mingling of wistfulness and motherly pride, she whispered to God, "Please watch over my little girl."

The train picked up speed and soon was gone from sight.

CHAPTER 9

Be still, and know that I am God.

Psalm 46:10 (KJV)

*D*aniel walked off across the yard in the pale light of dawn toward the barn. Ben, his old hound, trotted ahead of him, making his morning inspection of the place, pausing now and again to sniff, raising a leg here and there to mark his territory, his pee steaming in the cold air. The only other creatures stirring were the guineas, who were starting their descent, dropping to the ground in single file one behind the other, from where they had roosted high in an oak.

On past the barn stretched the field, now died off. Standing tranced in the early-morning fog, the outlying woods appeared as a silver-gray smudge on the landscape. Daniel paused at the gate and stood for a moment, gazing out at the scene before him. The bleak fields and barren woods, the somber tones of brown and gray—it all looked so still and quiet, beautiful in its own way, "for He hath made every thing beautiful in His time."

Daniel felt a sudden pang in his chest. Something about winter, its mood, had always pained a place somewhere deep in his soul, grieved some old wound, while yet at the same time lent an easing of sorts, a solace. It was a combination of poignancy and consolation, a place where he could either lose himself or find himself. Peculiar, that this would be his favorite time of year.

Suddenly, a cow bellowed, jerking his mind back.

He entered the stall and spoke softly to the cow, named Suzy by the children. "Mornin', Suzy, ol' girl." She turned and looked at him, twitching her tail and stomping one time, impatiently. He sat down on the squatty stool and blew on his hands to warm them, and with the bucket between his knees, he began milking. Streams of milk hit the tin pail, making a slight, pinging noise. As he milked, Daniel rested his head against Suzy's flank, her hide warm against his cheek. After a minute, as he sometimes did in that solitary time of the morning, he began praying out loud, convinced that the cow gave more readily, soothed by the words.

"Lord, I come before you this fine mornin' thankin' you for a restful night's sleep an' for lettin' me live to see another day. Thankyou, Lord, for my family an' all you give us. I humbly ask that you continue to bless us—" The cow shifted her weight and Daniel smiled. "An' bless Suzy."

"*Get up!*"

Daniel fell silent, and still, but his mind came fully alert. He had thought he was alone, but he had, just a moment ago, distinctly heard someone say something. The hairs stood up on the back of his neck as he then heard—no, *sensed* a presence behind him. He sat petrified in fear of what he believed was happening. Could the voice he heard really have been the voice of God, or was his mind just playing tricks on him? Just then, he felt a gentle movement of air behind him and heard a sound, a sort of rustling, like a swish of silk. *It's just the wind*, he told himself. But he was convinced otherwise, insomuch that he fully believed if only he could summon up the courage to turn around and look, he would surely lay eyes upon God's face, perhaps even be able to reach out and touch the hem of His garment. Daniel tried to imagine what He looked like, he wanted to turn around, but he couldn't move; he was too afraid.

Though it caused his heart to tremble in fear, Daniel exulted in the wonder of it. Hardly able to breathe, he held very still and waited for something phenomenal to happen. Keeping his face hidden, he stared at Suzy's teats as though in a trance, without really seeing them. His mouth felt as if it were wadded with cotton. Several interminable minutes passed...

But nothing happened.

Gradually, Daniel realized there was no one there. *He must have left*, he decided. *Probably just vanished into the air.*

Relaxing a little, he set the milk bucket aside. Slowly, he turned around to look. Nope, not a soul there but him and Suzy. He then got down on his hands and knees, and on all fours, he went over the ground, feeling with his palms flat, as though seeking some evidence that might prove that it had happened the way he thought it had. Drawing in a slow, deep breath, he thought, *God was standin' right here—on this very spot*. This was sacred ground. But then, common sense started creeping in, belying his confidence and making him doubt himself. His very next thought told him, *Man, you've gone slap crazy!* It was impossible. Nothing of the kind had really occurred; no such thing *could* occur. He looked all around. There was no burning bush, no silver cloud, just him and Suzy. The more he thought about it, he realized he had imagined the whole thing. There had been no voice, and nobody.

Daniel shook himself out of his reverie and stood up. Laughing aloud at his own absurdity, he went back to the stool and resumed milking. When he finished, he turned the cow out, then returned for the bucket. As he was filling an old pie tin with milk, four barn cats came running to claim it. At that instant, hunger asserted itself, and he heard his stomach rumbling. He left the barn, thinking only about grits and eggs, hot biscuits, and tomato gravy.

Now tinged with the rosy glow of sunrise, the morning fog was beginning to lift. Chickens scattering out of his way, Daniel headed back across the yard toward the house for breakfast, filled with a vague yearning he did not yet comprehend.

January 16, 1863

There's nothing ordinary about our days anymore. Life now compared to life as it used to be is as different as night and day. My heart trembles over what we hear is happening throughout the South. Just as I'd expected, the Yankees are proving themselves to be pure heathens—thieving, ignorant heathens at that. It's said they'll just invade a place, break in and steal whatever they want, and then when they're done with their ransacking and looting, they take an ax to anything left whole and chop it up, then set fire to it. They're said to be torching anything in their path that they can't cart away—houses, barns, cotton—and not a thing folks can do but stand by and watch while their blood, sweat, and tears go up in smoke. They're even desecrating graves looking for buried gold and silver. Pure fools! They're killing cows, hogs, and chickens, and leaving them to spoil. Just thinking of such wastefulness with folks having to grub and forage just to stay alive makes me want to scream. Not that I wish such evildoings on any of my fellow countrymen, but so far we've only heard of these things happening in big towns and on the big plantations, so maybe, with us being as off the beaten path as we are gives us some defense against such awfulness. May God keep us hid 'til the Yankees go home!

Though I know we're better off than some, especially them that's off fighting, it gets harder here every day. Even if we had money, there's nothing to buy. Coffee is scarce to none, and tea. And they want twenty-five cents for a pound of white sugar—high as a cat's back! And salt of all things has come more valuable than gold. We've still got meat—we're stretching what we have—and plenty of eggs, but we eat a lot of collards and corn bread. Thank goodness we each have a milk cow, so we do at least have milk and butter. (Butter is selling in town for seventy-five cents!)

I've hid some jars of seeds out in the woods, just in case, so me and Rachel can put in a garden come spring. And I've give up altogether on keeping the school going, now that so much of the work has fell on the young'uns.

As I read back over what I've just written, it seems impossible that anything of the kind could really be happening here on our own soil.

Again, God help us all.

CHAPTER 10

Deliver us from evil.

*—Matthew 6:13 (*KJV*)*

To live and die is complex enough, but to die in a manner that runs contrary to nature's enduring quest for survival makes for certain scandal and speculation, as in the death of Anna Bradley. Anna's drowning, an apparent suicide, had been shocking when it happened, and tragic, regardless of the fact that she had not been very well-liked she having been such a small-minded and crabbed sort of person. But that was four years ago, and time ticks on even if a clock isn't wound, and now, even among those who had been most closely associated with her, it was doubtful anyone really missed her any more, except maybe her daughter, Libby. Asher, Anna's husband, remarried a year after her death to a young widow named Penelope Scruggs. Penelope, who was nearly a decade younger than he, was good-natured and passionate, an accomplished cook, and true country girl—all virtues that Asher had lived largely without during the years he was married to Anna. A shy man around most, Asher was altogether different when he was with Penelope. Being with her made him seem more alive. It was like he had finally met the woman of his dreams. As for Libby, she held herself back from her stepmother, which was the way she usually did with people.

"You are good," Asher said to Penelope. "But you must be tired. I'll stay with her now; you go on to bed."

"I'm not all that tired," Penelope said valiantly, "but I would like to get my bath."

Libby had come home from school complaining of her head hurting. Penelope had not left her side for more than a few minutes all afternoon, sitting close beside her bed, keeping a cool rag on her forehead, holding her hand, and praying that something she did might, in some small way, help ease the girl's suffering. Whatever the cause for her violent, reoccurring headaches, they had not responded favorably to any of the remedies the doctor had prescribed, and if anything, they seemed to be occurring more frequently and worsening in severity.

The figure lying under the quilt was pale and delicate. Libby was fourteen, but she looked much younger, more like eleven or twelve, and she was immature in other ways too. Looking down at his sleeping child, Asher was anxious as to what to do. He felt helpless; he could hardly bear just sitting by, watching and waiting, when he knew his daughter was so obviously ill. Aside from the headaches, over the past months, her behavior had grown more and more puzzling as well. Libby had always been a quiet, private child, more so since the death of her mother it seemed, and most times lately her thoughts appeared altogether preoccupied, as though her mind was off in some faraway place, walled up in her own little world. Though she never talked about it, Anna's passing seemed to haunt the girl in a way that was hard to understand, considering there had been so little closeness between them. Anna had never loved Libby, and Libby knew it. Another thing Asher had noticed about his daughter was that she had become unreasonably fearful of people—men mostly, and particularly Hiram, who everyone knew wouldn't hurt a fly. Libby, nevertheless, acted skittish as a colt around him.

Asher was beginning to have serious concerns about Libby's state of mind. His worst fear was that she was becoming deranged, like Anna.

He stood and watched her as she lay sleeping. If only he could, he would make her better; he would give her his health, his strength—if only he could.

The clock on the wall sounded nine delicate chimes. Asher went then and stood before it, suddenly remembering how he had given Anna the timepiece on the first anniversary of their marriage. It was one of the few household items to survive the tornado that destroyed their old house some years back. He had built that house sound, solid, with the assumption it would always stand so, at least until long after his death. The thought had even crossed his mind that when the time came, Libby might have raised her own family within its walls. But that house was gone; it stood no more. A moment later, he moved away from the clock, vexed at having thought of all that now.

Nine o'clock. Libby had been asleep for almost five hours.

When Asher and Penelope were eating supper, it had started raining; it had come on harder as the hours passed. Asher looked toward the window and blinked his eyes. Drops of water slid down the panes like rivulets of sorrowful tears. Putting a hand to his face, he felt them. *Lord, what's the matter with my little girl?* he asked silently. Suddenly, he thought of Matt and Julie Robertson. Frightened for the life of his only child, he dropped to his knees and prayed, *O Lord, hear me, and have mercy on us, help us, forsake us not, for my soul trusts in thee. Heal Libby, O Lord, restore her body and her mind. Give me strength.* He was terrified of losing her.

When Asher finished praying, he stretched out in a chair and sat for a long while, watching the flickering flame from the lamp on the bedside table and listening to the rain dropping from the eaves of the house. Finally, his eyelids grew heavy, and he dozed off.

Libby began to hear the sounds around her. She could hear the creek, the faint ripple of the current as it slid downstream, the rush and cascade of it spilling over a submerged log. Sounds that threatened to take her to another world, her own private world, a place where she was trapped somewhere between reality and dreams. It was a place dark and forbidding, and sinister. Her stalker was there, in that dark world. She could not see his face, had never seen his face, but she could see his gruesome, claw-like hands. She went cold with fear as they started reaching for her. *Run!* Her nerves screamed, warning her to flee. She started running. *Running, running—he was chasing her. She had to keep running.*

With a gasp, Libby's eyes flew open, her pulse was racing. She looked quickly and fearfully about, searching the shadows of the room. Then she saw him. Though she could only vaguely make him out in the dim light, with a sigh of relief, she whispered, "Daddy." Outside, the wind was blowing. She could hear the rippling of leaves as it lifted the branches, the light patter of raindrops against the window. Gradually, she realized the sounds she'd heard had only come from the wind and the rain.

"Daddy?"

Asher woke at the sound of her voice. "Hey, sleepyhead," he said. "Daddy's right here." He reached out and took her hand. "How do you feel?"

"What happened, Daddy?" Her mind was so foggy she couldn't remember. She had no idea how long she had been sleeping.

He looked into her sleepy face and said, "You had another bad, bad headache this afternoon. Remember?"

"Uh-huh." She nodded. Now she remembered.

"You slept right through supper. You hungry?"

Libby shook her head drowsily. "No, sir. I just want to rest so I can go to school tomorrow. Miss Bernice doesn't like us skippin' lessons."

Asher smiled. "I'm sure Miss Bernice understands when you're sick." He leaned over and kissed her gently on the forehead. "I'm glad you're feelin' better. You sure there's nothin' I can get for you?"

She nodded. "I'm sure."

Relieved that the episode was over, he said, "Well then, I believe I'll turn in. I'll see you in the mornin'." As he tucked her covers in, he teased softly, "Sleep tight, don't let the bedbugs bite."

That brought a slight smile to Libby's face. She loved her daddy and wished she could tell him and make him understand about the voices that sometimes filled her head and about how she sometimes saw her mother's ghost. But there was no way to make him understand. How could he understand something he couldn't hear or see? She herself didn't understand. And telling him would only upset him, and she didn't want that. And she'd never be able to tell him about the man in the woods. He probably wouldn't believe her, anyway, and if he did, it would only make him worry more than he already did.

Libby's mind was all in a boggle. Everything was so confusing she didn't know what to do. But she did know that in some way, she was sick.

Asher went over and blew out the lamp. He started from the room but had gone only two steps when Libby's question stopped him.

"Daddy, am I going to die, like Belle?"

Asher did everything he could to fight back his tears. Grateful for the darkness so Libby couldn't see his face, he went back and, kneeling at the bed again, put his arms around her. He wanted to reassure her that everything was going to be all right, that she was going to be fine. *She had to be.* "No, sweetheart, Daddy won't let you die." After comforting her for a minute more, he touched her forehead again with his lips and wished her a good night.

His hand was reaching for the doorknob when Libby's voice made him pause again. "I'm sorry, Daddy." She didn't know why the words were coming to the surface now, but she couldn't hold them back any longer. She had to rid herself of her terrible guilt.

Asher turned back once more. "Honey, there's nothin' for you to be sorry about."

"Yes, there is, Daddy. Please don't be mad – " She started crying, her voice was barely more than a croak. "I killed Samuel's puppy...I held his head under the water an' drowned him in the creek."

CHAPTER 11

For the eyes of the Lord are over the righteous, and His ears are open unto their prayers; but the face of the Lord is against them that do evil.

—*1 Peter 3:12 (*KJV*)*

Nine hundred miles away, in the low, rolling hills of Virginia near the James River, Wilkes Graham had spent the entire day burning the brush off a newly cleared field, getting it ready to plow; in a few weeks when the conditions came right, he would plant it in tobacco. Despite the cool temperatures, his shirt had soaked through around the neck with sweat. Before he went into the house, he stripped it off and poured two dippers of water over his head from a bucket on the back porch and scrubbed the soot from his face and hands. Now, standing with his back to a crackling fire, he was rolling a glass of whiskey slowly between his palms. He was not drunk yet, but working his way there.

"I asked you a question, you stupid whore. Where'd you run off to today?" he growled.

The woman he was talking to was a twenty-year-old blonde named Louella Stinson, who had been living in a "house" on the outskirts of Richmond until Wilkes took her home with him on New Year's Eve. The house was brick, surrounded by a wall of cedars; it had its own little courtyard and gas lighting. There were a dozen other girls there, in a variety of sizes, ages, and colors. Louella had been one of the youngest, and she was still quite pretty. Wilkes had visited her in Richmond on a few occasions before New Year's Eve, and she had been flattered by his attention. He would take her little presents and was always very complimentary of her appearance. He made her feel beautiful, and special. Wilkes was something of a wealthy man, and devastatingly handsome and well-built. There was a careless, rugged air about him that women found irresistible. *And yet he chose me over all the others*, Louella would tell herself. She had always dreamed of meeting a man like him—rich, charming, *rich*. Wilkes was a true Southern gentleman.

Well, almost.

Louella had paid no attention to the warnings from some of the other girls who'd had dealings with Wilkes in the past. She hadn't wanted to hear about his bad temper or about how he sometimes took pleasure in the rough treatment of his women. *He's just a passionate man—intense*, she told herself, and believed it. When he had taken her home with him, though there were no promises made, she was confident—fool enough to believe— that Wilkes would someday fall madly in love with her and that he would eventually marry her and carry her over the threshold into a life of contentment and ease. That was seven weeks ago. Now, though she didn't like admitting it even to herself, she knew her hope of them becoming eternal lovebirds was never to grow wings.

Wilkes was indeed handsome, but Louella came to realize very soon there was much else about him that he kept hidden. Once she got to know him, she realized there were two men inside that irresistible body: one, kind and generous; the other, ruthless and cold—one whom she was hopelessly infatuated with, another whom she was terrified of. Sometimes living with Wilkes was like living with a wounded bear. He could be surly and unpredictable; she never knew when he might turn on her in a wild rage. He was controlling and had a tendency to be overly suspicious, especially when he'd had too much to drink. Over the course of time, all the warnings she'd ignored had come floating back to haunt her. They had all tried to tell her, but no, she refused to listen.

In retrospect, it seemed ironic to her that Wilkes had turned out to be so much like her own hard-drinking father, possessing the very same traits that made her flee his turbulent home as soon as she figured herself old enough to make it on her own. Remembering the dull misery on her mama's face, she thought about how she had sworn to herself time and again, *That will never be me.* Looking back, she reckoned she would have been as well off staying there with them, rather than be in the fix she was in now. Silently, she cursed her stupidity.

Louella had known the minute Wilkes came through the door that evening that he was in one of his dark moods. She sat with her eyes fixed on the floor, not daring to look him in the face, afraid of provoking him into becoming any angrier than he already was.

"I asked you where you went!" Wilkes yelled.

Louella felt a sense of foreboding flood through her. Her throat became dry and scratchy. She ran her tongue over her bottom lip to moisten it. "I told you," she answered in a soft, quavering voice, "I just went down the road to see Alice—just to girl-talk. I swear it." Alice McAndrews rented the house where Wilkes's former partner, Edward Douglas, had lived, before he sold out and moved with his wife, Lucy, to California. Originally, Hiram had built the house and lived there with his first wife, Madeline.

The room grew dangerously quiet; Louella's chest rose and fell in the silence. She could feel Wilkes staring at her, and each moment that passed seemed longer than the one before as she sat tense and waiting, quivering in her chair. In her mind, she started backing away, trying to brace herself for what was to come.

Wilkes drained the contents of his glass in one gulp and set it down on the table. Louella's heart gave a fearful leap as he started toward her. Saying nothing, he reached down and lifted her chin with his fist so that she was forced to meet his gaze. The coldness in his ice-blue eyes sent a chill through her. His scowl deepened as he watched her features like a hawk, as though he was trying to read her mind. She didn't have to remind herself how dangerous he could be.

"Ain't right," he said, "you go off without even botherin' to tell me. You ort-a know by now—I don't abide disrespect, 'specially from a slut like you." He seemed to get pleasure from belittling her.

As Louella looked at him, she felt a little queasy thinking how foolish she'd been to allow herself to fall prey to such an animal. Where in hell was all his charm now? Was he the penance for all her sins? Obviously she was not a religious sort, yet she did pray of finding a way out, a way of getting as far away from there and as far away from him as possible. She knew she had to escape somehow, but she had nowhere to go. And no one. If she were to go missing, not a soul would come looking for her—she knowing full well that Wilkes would have her skin, or worse, if he caught her trying to leave. She couldn't go back to the brothel. That's the first place he'd look. Right now, there was nowhere she could think of going where he wouldn't track her down. And she was penniless. She'd think of something, but for now, she had no choice but to play the game.

"I-I was wrong to go there—anywhere for that matter—without tellin' you…I'm sorry, really. I didn't mean to upset you… it's just that I get so lonely stayin' shut up in this big ol' house all day with no one to talk to. Sometimes I feel like climbin' the walls." Her eyes met his meaningfully. "Surely you can understand that."

There was something provocative in her voice, something unexpected that made Wilkes pause. He stared at her for a long moment, his jaw seeming to relax somewhat. Admittedly, the wench was something to look at. And her experience in bed did prove entertaining. None to gently, he ran his thumb across her lips and traced the outline of her mouth. Her lips were full, pink, tempting...

At the end of what seemed like an eternity, he laughed softly in his mocking way. "Damn, Louella, if you ain't a handful—in more ways than one." Feeling a quickening in his loins, he slid his hands boldly over her body and leaned toward her, pausing when their lips were a fraction of an inch apart. Trembling, Louella waited for his kiss. But Wilkes drew back slightly, toying with her. After a long moment, he whispered against her hair, speaking deliberately slow and precise, "Be mighty unfortunate if you was to try an' sneak off from me." Louella closed her eyes tightly as his mouth swooped down hard upon hers, his kiss insistent and possessive, devouring, smothering...

Later on, while Wilkes slept like he was drugged, Louella lay in his arms contentedly, with her head on his chest. She had never felt so happy. All was now forgotten except how Wilkes had made her feel—beautiful, special. Now, in her mind she defended him. She was convinced that all he'd said before had just been an act. Like most men, Wilkes needed to be dominant. It had been ridiculous for her to fear him. He was the most wonderful man she'd ever met, and there was no doubt whatsoever in her mind that he would ever intentionally hurt her. If he didn't care for her, she rationalized, why would he have brought her there to live with him in the first place?

Sometime during the night, Louella became startled. She rolled over onto her back and lay still for a minute, listening. She thought she'd heard something or at least sensed something—

some kind of movement—close to her face. It felt like someone had touched her, or like something was crawling on her head. She ran her fingers through her hair. Or had she just imagined it? No. There it was again! Something just grazed the side of her head! Actually, it was more like a slight, sharp blow. Dear God, what was that? A bird?

As her eyes adjusted to the darkness, she could make it out, and what she saw made her blood go cold. It was hovering over her, a few feet over the bed, like some evil, malignant spirit. It was staring at her intently, its glassy eyes glowing demonically, like two red coals.

Louella was paralyzed with fear. Cowering beneath the sheet, she tried to cry out for help, but the sound froze in her throat. With trembling hands, very carefully she reached for the quilt and slowly started pulling it higher, hoping it might offer some protection against the hideous creature.

Suddenly without warning, the enormous hawk swooped down on her! Louella put her arms up in a desperate attempt to fend it off, but it lit on her face. She couldn't breathe! It was suffocating her, smothering her with its huge wings, scratching her face with its claws! She fought wildly, unable to fathom how such a thing could be happening. The hawk began pecking her! It pierced her skin with its sharp beak, ripping her flesh apart. There was blood dripping from her arms. The hawk was devouring her, literally eating her alive! The pain was excruciating, the horror unspeakable! Inside her head, she began to scream. She screamed again and again until, finally, she woke herself.

Louella was in a cold sweat. Her body was trembling, her heart racing. Her eyes darted around the room in a panic. It took her a few minutes to get her bearings and realize it was all just a terrible nightmare. With that thought, slowly she began to relax a little. She sank back onto her pillow and closed her eyes, feeling the tension drain out of her body. As she lay there, she tried to concentrate on other things, pleasant things, to calm her nerves.

Just when she was starting to feel better, Wilkes stirred slightly in his sleep. In that moment, Louella's eyes flew open as another, more horrifying thought struck her. *Devouring...smothering.* Hardly moving for fear of waking him, she very slowly, very cautiously turned her head to look at him. Raven-black hair, a slight hook just below the bridge of his nose—even in the dim light, there was an evil, hawkish look about him.

That's when Louella knew for certain. Her nightmare was real—and lying right next to her.

CHAPTER 12

The Lord is good, a stronghold in the day of trouble; and He knoweth them that trust Him.

*—Nahum 1:7 (*KJV*)*

" Would anyone care for a piece of pie with their coffee?" Laura asked.

There was a collective shaking of heads and replies of "No, thank you" and "Coffee's fine" around the table. It was only nine o'clock in the morning, too soon after breakfast for them to be hungry, and they each were more interested in finding out why Asher had called them all together. They knew it had to be something important. He had asked Hiram and Addie to meet with him and Penelope at Wesley and Laura's house, and presently everyone was gathered around the table in Laura's kitchen. She brought a pot of coffee from the stove and started pouring it into cups. Before she sat down, she set a coconut pie before them, just in case anyone were to change their mind.

The expression on Asher's face was serious unto solemn, his eyes deeply troubled. He looked and felt as though he were carrying the weight of the world on his shoulders. He had lain awake all night, thinking about Libby, worrying about what lay ahead for her. Conscious that everyone was waiting on him to say something, he took a deep breath and began with, "I know I'm hinderin' y'all from other things this mornin', but we're all family here, an' what I need to discuss with you is a family matter."

While they listened, he explained, "Libby's sick. She's been sick for some time now, an' from all indications, she's getting sicker." They all looked at him with instant concern, but they recognized the importance of letting him finish what he set out to tell. "It was a bad thing for her, to lose her mama at such a young age...an' in such a manner..." His voice trailed off for a minute. "I've seen a difference in Libby ever since Anna died. I reckon I just figured with time, she'd get better...but then the headaches started; she came home from school sick again day before yesterday. An' *now*, she's told me she *sees* Anna sometimes—sees her...*ghost*."

In a matter-of-fact tone, Laura said, "Asher, you know as well as I do, Libby's always been...well, a little strange, and all children have wild imaginations. That's perfectly normal." Then thinking about how that must have sounded, she quickly said, "I didn't mean that in an ugly way. I love Libby; you know I do."

A sad smile touched Asher's eyes. "I know you do," he replied charitably. "Libby's my daughter, therefore I do know as well as anyone she's always been thought to be, as you say, *a little strange*." She was also precious, at least to him. In his eyes, Libby was a gift from God. And, strange or not, Anna's suicide had exacerbated Libby's problems. Anna's suicide had had an emotional effect on him, so understandably it had affected Libby. He remembered at the time wondering what had made Anna kill herself. Was she so unhappy? Had her suicide somehow been his fault? Had Anna loved him? Ever? There had been questions in his mind, but no answers. But work had taken his mind off his feelings. He was busy rebuilding their house. Then Penelope came into his life. As he looked back now, a shadow of misgiving crossed his heart as he realized that Libby had to have been struggling with the same difficult questions. But he had been so busy trying to provide for her physically that he had failed her, at least, emotionally. "Unfortunately, it's much more serious than that," he said.

He continued, "The doctor examined Libby before, when she first started having the headaches, an' he gave her some medicine. But after what all she told me the other night, I went back and talked to him again yesterday, without her there." He felt a lump rise in his throat. His voice became raw with emotion. "After I told him about what happened with Anna, he told me that Libby...he said it's *possible* that Libby might have inherited some sort of mental illness from Anna. He said she needs to see a specialist...somebody trained to deal with problems like hers—a psychiatrist. He went so far to say that without treatment, she could even end up in an asylum." His eyes filled with tears at the thought. And when might this happen, he'd asked the doctor—a year from now, five years, ten? No one knew. There was no way of knowing. He shook his head and brought his hands to his face. "I could never put my little girl in a place like that." He was trusting in God that would never happen.

"An *asylum!*" Laura cried. "Why, that's nonsense! Libby's not *insane*...surely he's wrong. There must be something..."

The look in Asher's eyes silenced her. There was more. Something almost too awful to tell. When Libby had told him, he'd felt a rush of sadness so profound, it shocked him.

"Libby told me she killed Samuel's puppy, drowned him in the creek."

Everyone at the table went completely still. Not one eye blinked. Nothing could have prepared them for that detail. As the image of it burned across their brains, they could do nothing but stare at him. It was shocking, disturbing. Unthinkable. Children didn't drown puppies. Hiram and Wesley exchanged a glance, both remembering the day they were splitting wood, buzzards had flown over, they had gone into the woods, the puppy was on the creek bank—dead.

After an interminable silence, Laura said, "Aw, Libby probably just made that up...for attention...you know how children do sometimes." But gradually it was coming to her—to them all—that Libby was ill, seriously ill.

Asher shook his head sorrowfully. "She wouldn't lie about that. I believe her." He sounded so forlorn when he said, "I've turned it over in my mind a hundred times...I don't know what to do or where to start." He felt as though he was walking through a maze, blindfolded.

Everyone sat looking grave, pondering and sorting the situation in their minds. Their hearts went out to him and Penelope and to Libby. They were filled with concern and wanted to reassure them, but no one knew what to say. For a fact, it made them all conscious of how blessed they were not to have such worries.

As the silence in the room lengthened, Addie stood up and took her cup to the sink. She looked silently out the window, her mind working. An intricately spun spiderweb spanned the distance between two crepe myrtles. Raindrops from the night before clung to its silvery threads like strings of crystal beads and shimmered in the morning light. A she stared at it, suddenly, an idea came to her. It was the obvious and logical solution. *Travis.* Travis was on staff at one of the largest hospitals in the country. An old and trusted friend, surely, he could advise them. She knew he would do whatever he could to help them. She turned around and asked Asher, "Have you thought about contacting Travis? If anyone can help Libby, he probably can, or at least might know someone who can."

That had not occurred to Asher. It seemed like a good idea. *But Travis is in Memphis. How could we possibly—*

It was as though Addie read his thoughts. She said, "With God all things are possible. I'll write to him myself, if you like, and explain it all as best I can. It couldn't hurt."

Thought by all to be an excellent idea, Asher expressed his gratitude to Addie and agreed. So it was settled: she would send a letter to Travis the very next day.

When Addie went to the post office the following morning, there was a letter from Emily. To no surprise, she was adapting well to her life on campus at the college. She liked her teachers and enjoyed all her classes, making high marks in every subject, of course. Seemingly, she and her dorm mate had much in common and went everywhere together. She had also taken a part-time job at a variety store near the school, with hopes of working there full-time during the summer, to save every penny she could before the fall semester began. To hear Emily tell it, the sophistication of Hattiesburg rivaled that of New York City. Her excitement and happiness over this new phase of her life was evident, which eased Addie's mind tremendously.

"I still can't believe I'm actually here," she wrote. "It all still seems like a wonderful, incredible dream."

CHAPTER 13

Not that I speak in respect of want, for I have learned, in whatsoever state I am, therewith to be content.

—Philippians 4:11 (KJV)

Flags flying, with tiered decks gleaming white and turrets trimmed with gingerbread, she was grand, a queen among peasants compared to every other vessel on the river. Great plumes of steam roiled from her twin smokestacks; her giant paddlewheel propelled the muddy water, leaving a trail of foam in her wake. Travis stood gazing out his fourth-floor office window watching the riverboat navigate the spellbinding currents of the Mississippi, thinking about how much he loved living in Memphis—and about how much he missed his old life in Oakdale.

Had it been only two years, two years already, since he and Abigail had moved here? As he pondered it, he remembered his excitement when his son, Brandon, had first told him about the position at Shelby County Memorial, and Abigail's excitement as they formulated plans to move. Abigail had always felt more at home in the city.

Nowadays, he had a renewed closeness with Brandon and his daughter-in-law, Serena, and he found great joy in his two grandchildren. His work at the hospital was immensely gratifying; great strides were being made in the field of medicine, and he considered himself fortunate to serve alongside some of the country's most revered physicians. Abigail's position at the bank was as important to her as his at the hospital was to him, and she was a zealous member of the prestigious Nineteenth Century Club, a philanthropic and cultural organization that promoted the advancement of women. They both enjoyed the beat and bustle of the city. Memphis was a cornucopia of history, music, restaurants, clubs, and shops.

And yet still…, Travis thought.

Given his genuine concern for the well-being of people, and a keen interest in the simple and ordinary business of their lives, it was only natural that a certain amount of wistfulness came upon Travis when he looked back over his years as a small-town country doctor. Sometimes he truly missed that role, and especially the people and the undefined relationships, those that no one tried to put a word on as to what they were. Those had been happy times for him, sometimes he thought his happiest. Sad, he sometimes thought, that time couldn't be recaptured. It made him sad, sometimes, knowing that those particular times would never be his again.

Then, shifting his thoughts back to Addie's letter and what she had written about his successor, Travis couldn't help but chuckle. It seemed that the whole town liked the new doctor—they were just having trouble keeping a straight face when saying his name. Understandably so. Apparently, he was a good sport about it, though, and took the ribbing all in fun. Addie wrote that he declared to having cured more patients with laughter than with medicine. Travis had no doubt as to that being true as he thought, what were the chances? Odder still, what chance had there been that the man should end up married to a woman named Minnie? Just to amuse himself, he said it aloud. "Dr. Waymore Killings and his wife, Minnie Killings." It was easy to see why they were all in hysterics.

Shaking his head, Travis turned from the window and returned to his desk. He picked up Addie's letter and began rereading it for the third time, skipping past the hospitable salutations and general news focusing expressly on the passage about Libby:

> What I tell you now is on behalf of Laura's brother, Asher, and I must say this is very difficult for me to put it into words. I hardly know where to begin or what is pertinent to tell you.
>
> Of course you will remember that Asher's first wife, Anna, drowned herself. His daughter, Libby, is now fourteen years old, though you would not guess it. It distresses me to inform you that, according to Asher, the girl's behavior has come increasingly bizarre, insomuch that he and Penelope are in a state of despair and desperation as to what to do.
>
> Libby is plagued by terrible, debilitating headaches. And although she has always been somewhat of a strange child, Asher said, of late, she seems more withdrawn and more timid around certain people—men in particular, he said. Notably Hiram, if you can imagine anyone could possibly feel uncomfortable around him.
>
> Libby claims to have seen Anna's ghost on several occasions, and that Anna has spoken to her. And that is not even the worst of it. She has admitted to drowning Samuel's defenseless little puppy in the creek! She said this happened a few months after Anna's death.
>
> Dr. Killings is sure he has done all he can do for the poor girl. He has even mentioned to Asher the possibility of having her committed to an institution if her condition continues to worsen.
>
> So, on behalf of Asher, I am issuing a plea for you to consider a referral for Libby and assistance in arranging

travel for her to go to Memphis where she might be evaluated by a doctor specifically trained to treat those with her type of problem. I realize this is a lot to ask, but I have every confidence in you, as a doctor and as a friend. Bear in mind, Asher is a farmer, and the planting seasoning is all but upon us. (Tell me, where does the time go?)

We are awaiting your response and will be forever obliged for any advice you can impart and for whatever assistance.

Please give Abigail my best.

With warmest regards for my old and dear friend,

Addie

Travis laid the letter aside and took a cigar from the box on his desk. He settled back, tilting his chair onto its hind legs. Closing his eyes, he tried to call up an image of the girl Libby in his mind. Instead, charged by an unexpected resurgence of old dreams and secret longings, the only face he saw was Addie's. He missed her, *his friend*. Unbeknown to any save himself, Addie had spent half her life in and out of his thoughts, and thinking of her now suddenly made him feel lonely. Rolling the cigar between his fingers, he found himself wondering what hope there was of her ever coming to Memphis. He sniffed the cigar and bit off the end.

There was a time when Travis had wished for impossible things—a time when he had, in the recesses of his heart, coveted another man's wife for his own. Addie was the love of his life, this he acknowledged freely—that is, freely within the confines of his own mind.

One day long ago, *the day of the fire*, it had finally become evident, *he had asked her to marry him*, a solid understanding had come to him, *she said no*, he would never be worthy of such a love with her. Now and again over the years, unbidden thoughts would come into his mind, and he had had to remind himself that a person couldn't have everything in life. Some things just weren't meant to be. *Nonetheless, life's been good*, he told himself.

Life is good. Despite his disappointment that Addie had rejected his proposal, he was content enough, happy enough, just in his knowing that Hiram cherished her above all else in this world.

Travis lit the cigar and drew on it deeply.

Addie was happily married and in love with Hiram; Hiram held her heart. And Travis was married to Abigail; Abigail was an extraordinarily beautiful, intelligent, and spirited woman, and Travis admired and respected her. And theirs was a good marriage, maybe not in the way of fireworks, but a good marriage. They were well suited to each other, they were devoted partners.

Travis exhaled, releasing a big billow of smoke. *Thus it was, and thus it would always be...*

Again: Travis was not unhappy. He could claim no real regret. *...thus confounding the romantics.*

The senior psychiatrist on staff at Shelby Memorial Hospital was Dr. Stephen Alexander. Highly respected in his field, he was in his forties, tall, with prematurely gray hair and compassionate, hazel eyes. Although a very distinguished-looking and confident man, there was a terminal dishevelment about his appearance that came as a result of working too many hours, for too many years. In his business, there was always a patient to see, always a report to write, always a meeting to attend; it was a way of life for him, part of his soul, and he loved it.

His was a spacious office with a spectacular view of the Mississippi River. The room was richly paneled and tastefully furnished, though somewhat untidy. There were framed credentials and paintings on the walls, and shelves filled with gold-embossed leather books. But there were also books stacked on chairs and medical journals strewn across the desk and floor, and several potted plants. The overall effect was an inviting, lived-in atmosphere that felt more like a home than an office. Essentially, it was a comfortable space in which he could work.

Dr. Alexander was the first friend Travis had made after moving to Memphis, and now it seemed they had always been friends. At least once a week, he and his wife, Miranda, went to dinner with Travis and Abigail, sometimes the only meal Miranda and he shared in a week due to his demanding schedule. They were used to it, though; they had lived that way for twenty years. Thankfully, she, like Abigail, understood that she had married a doctor as well as a man, and, the two women often went shopping together to pass the time, when their husbands couldn't break away from the hospital.

The receptionist had gone to lunch, and the door was open when Travis came around the corner. Knocking, he poked his head in and said, "Anyone home?"

Dr. Alexander looked up. He had been waiting for Travis. "Come in," he greeted him. "Take a seat."

Travis sat down across from him and took two cigars from his breast pocket. Getting right to the business that had brought him there, he said, "So tell me. What did you think about the letter?"

After lighting his cigar, Dr. Alexander leaned back in his chair and clasped his hands behind his head. "I'm intrigued. This Libby sounds like a fascinating child." *A fascinating study.*

"Well, based on what you read, what's your opinion?" Travis asked.

Dr. Alexander hesitated for a moment. "Well, as you have just stated, anything I say at this point would be nothing more than conjecture and theory. It would be impossible to form a conclusive diagnosis without actually sitting down and talking with the girl and procuring a more in-depth history." He was too good a psychiatrist to make a judgment of that kind without having sufficient information. "However, based on the behaviors described by your friend, I'd say the child is quite obviously acting out, most likely in fear, because of some traumatic event in her life. My guess is that her headaches, in all likelihood, are caused from the stress of that fear."

Travis nodded. "By traumatic event, you mean her mother's suicide." It was a statement, not a question.

Dr. Alexander replied, "Her mother's death might possibly play a part. Grief is a major stressor. However, I find it highly improbable that in itself would cause an adolescent girl to drown a puppy." He looked at Travis thoughtfully for a moment. Travis was a friend and respected colleague. He knew he could trust him. Otherwise, he would never make such a bold presumption without having concrete proof. "It's what was said about the girl's uneasiness around men that raised a flag of caution in my mind." He took a deep draw from his cigar and held the pungent smoke in his mouth for a long moment. After exhaling, he said, "Off the record, my fundamental impression is that Libby is a victim of carnal molestation. Most likely by someone closely affiliated with the family."

Dr. Alexander could see that Travis was completely taken aback. Knowing that he had close ties with that family, he could only guess what he was thinking. He ventured to ask, "How well do you know the man Hiram?"

Travis wanted desperately not to believe what Dr. Alexander alluded to. It was inconceivable, illogical. *I don't believe it…it can't be true. Be he undeniably a brilliant psychiatrist, Stephen is wrong this time.* As Travis sat there rolling it over in his mind, he was aware that Stephen's eyes never left his face. But this was a matter he needed to muse on in private, when he was alone. Giving nothing away, he asked, "Do you think you can help her?"

Dr. Alexander had already looked at his calendar; his schedule was completely booked for weeks, his case load full. Only the day before, he had turned a new patient away and referred her to an associate. Nevertheless, the prospect of treating this girl filled him with a great sense of anticipation. Sick as it might seem, Libby Bradley was every psychiatrist's dream patient. What horrible thing had happened to her? What horrible thing *was* happening to her? What had she experienced in her young life to make her so afraid, so unable to cope in a normal way? He suspected that Libby had all the answers locked away somewhere inside her psyche, and with God's blessing, he wanted to help her, free her, if at all possible. It was just the sort of thing he lived for.

"Can you arrange for her to come to Memphis?"

CHAPTER 14

There is that scattereth, and yet increaseth...

—Proverbs 11:24 (KJV)

"Hate I'm late." It was a few minutes past six when Daniel entered the woodshop. "Ol' Ben's up an' turned sick."

Hiram was hitching the horses. Giving Daniel a questioning look, he asked, "What you reckon's wrong with him?" He knew Daniel thought the world of Ben. Back in his youth, he too had loved a dog in such a way.

Daniel shook his head. "Beats me. He seemed fine last night, but when I went out to feed him a while ago, he was actin' funny. He just lay there, wouldn't hardly lift up his head. Thumped his tail a time or two but wouldn't eat or drink a thing...an' that ain't like Ben." Ben was a typical hound dog, greedy to the bone.

"You check him for ticks?" Hiram asked.

Daniel nodded. "Didn't find a one. Felt all around on his neck, looked in his ears—they cleaner than mine. No sign of snakebite, 'course it's a little early for snakes to be stirrin'."

"He might be wormy."

Another shake of the head. "Ain't been three weeks I treated him for worms. I thought he might've got into somethin' dead, ate some carrion. He weren't pukin', though, didn't have the scours."

"Might just be old age. Ben must be…how old, you reckon?" Hiram well remembered the day way back yonder when Daniel and the dog had been reunited. It was years ago, on the day he and Addie first met, the day of her mother's funeral. That day, Addie had sent the dog home with Wesley. At the time Daniel was living with Wesley and Laura and working as Hiram's apprentice. Hiram had been aware all that summer of Daniel's troubled spirits, but he had not known the reason, only that it had something to do with his father. He had not known then, that except in a biological way, Daniel had no father. All Hiram knew was that Daniel, like all boys, needed friending by a man. He needed to be shown and taught a real man's ways, a godly man's ways, and Hiram did that. And in time, without having set out to do so, *he* had become Daniel's father.

With a frown, Daniel considered the question. "Hmmm…let me see. I'd say Ben's getting' on eleven, maybe twelve years."

"Dang-it!" Hiram said. "That'd make him about eighty in dog years. If I live to be that old, I 'spect I'll act funny too."

Grinning cockily, Daniel said, "Shoot, old man. Ben's just now fixin' to hit his prime, same as me!" He did a quick bob-and-weave and slugged Hiram on the shoulder in a jesting way.

Hiram grunted at his nonsense and replied drily, "How 'bout you help this old man get this cabinet loaded. We plannin' to make it to Ellisville an' back before dark, we best get a move on." Though they had been given a mild day for the trip, it was the third week of February, still winter, and the days were short.

The cabinet was the one commissioned by Miss Bernice's cousin. It was packed in a wooden crate, and was very heavy, with glass doors. Hiram was a strong man, but he anticipated it would take considerable muscle, and a fair share of savage cursing, to get it onto the wagon. And he was right. Though it didn't take them long, it was strenuous work, and when they were done, Daniel's arms were aching.

When the crate was secured to his satisfaction, Hiram stepped over the back of the seat and took up the reins. Daniel was leaning forward on the seat beside him, still trying to catch his wind. He marveled to himself at the ease in which Hiram had picked up his side of the crate. With a bit more humility, he exclaimed, "That son-of-a-gun must weigh a ton!"

As he slapped the horses' backs, Hiram threw his head back and laughed. With eyes crinkling, he couldn't resist saying, "Who's the old man now?"

During the Civil War, Jones County had been a haven for deserters of the Confederacy and the setting for an entity hailed as the "Free State of Jones"—a plan of secession led by a notorious rebel named Newt Knight. Until recently, the town of Ellisville, which was established in 1826, had been the county's judicial seat. In 1906, however, Jones County was redistricted and now had two seats: one at Ellisville and a second at the nearby lumber town of Laurel.

In good time, Hiram and Daniel arrived at the home of Charlotte Adams. Located on the main road between Ellisville and Laurel, hers was a noble house made of red brick; its trim and shutters were painted white, the trunks of the trees nearest the house, whitewashed. A seat was built around the base of an oak; rows of narcissus and daffodils bordered the porch and walkway. Charlotte and her late husband, Joel, had settled into the home after she inherited it from her parents, she being their only surviving child, her brother having died in the war. A town man through and through, Joel Adams had studied law and leaned toward politics; he and Charlotte had been a happy, loving pair, and naturally they had wanted children. Charlotte bore two daughters, two pretty little girls named Francis and Idelle. However, as it transpired, during the winter of 1871, both girls fell ill and died from pneumonia; Francis had been seven, her little sister, five. After Joel's death, Charlotte had never considered remarrying and was presently an aging widow in her midsixties.

As they pulled the wagon near the house, the front door opened, and Charlotte hurried out to stand on the porch. She had been watching for them from the window. Raising both hands in the air, she exclaimed, "Oh, here you are!" She stepped forward to greet them and introduced herself. "I'm Charlotte Adams, and you must be Mr. Graham." She had smiling, blue eyes and was wearing a dress that almost matched them perfectly. Her only jewelry was the gold band on her finger.

Hiram replied respectfully, "Yes, ma'am. I'm pleased to meet you. I'm Hiram Graham, and this is my son, Daniel Coulter."

Looking Daniel over, she said, "My, you are the handsomest thing I've seen in a long while!"

Daniel blushed and grinned. For an instant, he thought there was something about her that seemed familiar, but he didn't have time to ponder it, for Charlotte said, "Surely y'all would like some refreshment. You must be tired and hungry after traveling all morning and halfway across the state to get here. Excuse me while I go tell Claudia that our guests have arrived."

"Ma'am, not to sound impolite, but if it's all the same to you, we'd rather tend to the business of the cabinet first," Hiram said. They were anxious to get it unloaded.

"Very well then, if you're sure, come, and I'll show you where I'd like it put," Charlotte replied. "Quite frankly, I can hardly wait to see it myself."

The house was lavishly furnished and smelled of lemon, baking bread, and sunshine. Charlotte ushered them across polished floors and Oriental carpets, through the main parlor and down a long hallway into a smaller, cozier sitting room. There was a piano near the window, a writing desk, and a table bearing books, sewing notions, and embroidery frames. In a corner was a glass curio, filled with a collection of porcelain dolls; another held dozens of snow globes. "This is the room we enjoy the most," she chirped gaily. "Isn't it, Sydney dear?" Hiram and Daniel glanced at each other at the same time uncomprehendingly, until they spied a fluffy, white cat curled up on the velvet-upholstered sofa. The pampered puss sported a wide, sparkly collar around its neck. Forsaking his manners, Daniel dug an elbow into Hiram's side, a smile playing around his mouth. Never before had he been in such a fancy place! It was almost like walking through a store, or a museum.

Off the sitting room was the dining room, and after being shown where Charlotte wanted the china cabinet set, it was determined the most logical way to bring it into the house was along a brick pathway that led to a side door, which opened into the storeroom behind the kitchen. While passing through the kitchen, Charlotte introduced the men to Claudia, an amiable colored woman who generally cooked and helped Charlotte keep the house; Claudia's husband was Charlotte's groundskeeper.

Once again, moving the heavy cabinet proved to be an ordeal, but once it was uncrated and put in place, Charlotte exclaimed that she had never laid eyes on anything more beautiful—a triumph for the one who built it, a victory indeed for those who had wrestled with it.

As Hiram and Charlotte stood talking, Daniel let himself drift over to her old cabinet, which was actually more of a cupboard. He was looking at it good and hard when Charlotte noticed him. She went over and said, "This piece once belonged to one of Joel's relatives...an aunt, I believe." She paused to remember. "Ah yes.

His aunt Edith. Joel always said that God broke the mold after he made her. Prim-looking, little lady with blue hair. A bit daft—so as not to say *giddy*." Her eyes dared Daniel to finish the thought for her before she actually whispered the words "wine bibber." She smiled at Daniel in a teasing way. "Of course, staunch Baptist she was, to hear her *tell* it, you'd think it was a sin punishable by God to simply sniff a cork!" She laughed good-naturedly, and Daniel couldn't help laughing with her.

With a cheerful sigh, Charlotte turned her attention back to the old cupboard. "Not a thing wrong with this one," she said. "It's quite nice actually. It just no longer suits my needs." Her collection of ironstone had simply outgrown it.

Daniel made no reply but nodded agreeably.

After weighing the matter in her mind for a moment, she said, "I hope you won't take offense, this being a cast-off and you being a craftsman yourself and all, but do you think your wife might have use for it?"

Daniel felt the blood rush to his face and neck. "Oh no, ma'am, no offense taken…an'…it's Hiram who's the true craftsman here…I just pretty much help him…an', yes, ma'am, Amelia could probably come up with a hundred uses for it, but I couldn't—"

Judging by his stammering response, Charlotte knew, or at least guessed, what he must be thinking, *money*, so she quickly explained. "I only mean—it's plain to see there's far too much clutter in this house to stumble over as it is. What's the point in me stowing it in the attic to simply collect dust if someone might have use for it, and enjoy it? To be honest, you'd be doing me a favor, a great service actually, if you'd just take it off my hands so I wouldn't have to fool with it."

Still, Daniel felt awkward. "Mrs. Adams, I really couldn't…it belonged to your husband's aunt."

Charlotte waved a hand. "Posh. It's not like she was his *favorite* aunt." She would not be refused. She had no heirs, no one to leave her estate to. That, and moreover, she liked Daniel and wanted him to have it. She said, "God allowed our paths to cross for a reason, and for all we know, this could perfectly well be it. So that settles it."

Daniel said his thanks, and he and Hiram loaded the cupboard onto the wagon. Charlotte then showed them where they could wash up. When they returned to the kitchen and had taken seats at the table, Claudia set down a tray laden with fresh-baked bread, thick slices of ham and cheese, and pickles. A moment later, she returned carrying a pot of coffee, its spout steaming delectably. Next came a lemon meringue pie. Claudia had a special knack for making sweets and had taken great pains to get the meringue just right. It was light as air and browned to perfection. And everyone knew nothing tastes better with coffee than lemon meringue pie.

"God in heaven, that pie looks good!" Daniel exclaimed, which made Charlotte and Claudia smile in a satisfied way. Charlotte could see why Bernice had spoken so highly of the men. Everything about them suggested that they were good people, and she couldn't help warming to them both. Their company had brought a bright spot to what otherwise would have been a long and ordinary day.

"I've always contended a sweet tooth is a blessed thing," she said. "If my dear, departed Joel had eaten more pie and less pork, he'd no doubt be sitting here with us right now."

They ate and talked, the men doing most of the eating, Charlotte doing most of the talking. And just when they declared they could eat no more, Hiram and Daniel had another piece of pie. Afterward, Charlotte and Hiram went into the library to finalize their business. Reaching into a drawer, she withdrew an envelope that contained payment for the cabinet. She stood on one side of the desk, Hiram on the other, as he counted the money. When he had finished, he looked over at her, but before he could say anything, Charlotte said, "I'm sure the amount is accurate."

But Hiram found it to be more than the agreed-upon sum. "Ma'am—" he started.

Charlotte quickly reached over and touched his hand to stop him. "Please, Mr. Graham…" Her voice was earnest. "I believe God blesses us so we can be a blessing to others. As my dear mother used to say, 'It's not what you gather, but what you scatter that really matters.' That aside, the cabinet exceeds my grandest expectations, and you've come quite far to deliver it. You truly do deserve a little something extra for all your trouble."

All of a sudden, Charlotte felt uncharacteristically tired and old, and lonelier than she had felt in a long time. For a moment, her mind drifted as she thought about Joel and their two little girls…Once, way back, her life had seemed like a dream come true. But that was all so long ago, so long ago in fact, she sometimes wondered if it had only been a dream. She realized that she was feeling sorry for herself, and scolded herself for it. She supposed she should be thankful for all God had given her, and she was, but she would trade it all if only she could turn back the hands of time and have her family back. The feeling of loss, the longing to see them again—it never went away. It had become part of her. She had just learned to live with it. Smiling wistfully, she said, "It would do this old woman's heart good if you'd accept it as a token of my appreciation."

Hiram was touched by her kindness, and her giving spirit. He could see that it was very important to her that he accept the bonus. And he understood why. The way her eyes had misted over when she'd talked about her family earlier – she had so much, yet she had nothing. She was surrounded by the finest things that money could buy, but beneath the wealthy veneer, deep inside her heart, she suffered the sorrows of loneliness. He said, "This is very generous of you, Mrs. Adams, an' I'm much obliged. You an' Mrs. Claudia have been a blessing to me today." He folded the envelope and put it in his pocket.

Charlotte smiled, feeling very pleased and happy again. Leaving the library, she and Hiram made their way up the center hall and found Daniel in the front parlor, playing with an abacus.

He immediately stopped and stood up when they came in, looking embarrassed at being caught. Addressing them both, Charlotte said, "Now, I meant what I said. If it ever comes handy for y'all to come back this way, I'll treat you to dinner at the Alice Hotel in Ellisville. They serve a peach pie à la mode that is simply *divine!*"

Once outside, they all exchanged final thanks and farewells. Claudia handed Hiram a sack of sandwiches and cookies and a jar of sweet tea for the long ride home; Daniel climbed aboard holding a doll and a toy replica of a car that Charlotte insisted he take and give to Rachel and Carson.

With near regret, the women watched the wagon pull away.

The very moment the wheels rolled from the private drive onto the main road, Daniel said, "When I first walked in that house an' seen all them fancy things, an' that sissified cat, I said to myself, 'Country has come to town,' but that Mrs. Adams back there is one nice lady, Mrs. Claudia too. An' Amelia's gonna have a fit when she sees that cupboard." It was almost like Christmas morning. He leaned back and commenced to picking his teeth with a broom straw. After a thoughtful moment, he said, "An' you don't have to say I said so—Mrs. Adams bein' so much older an' all—but I swear there was somethin' about her that reminded me of Mama."

Hiram considered it for a minute. "Probably just her ways," he said. "Like you said, she's one nice lady." Though she had more money than she'd ever need, there was nothing pretentious about Charlotte Adams. She had gone above and beyond to make them feel welcome. Then a minute later, something Hiram had almost forgotten suddenly came back to him. "I did happen to notice that she has the same color eyes as your ma."

The sun was just sinking below the line of hardwoods beyond the barn when Daniel arrived home. Amelia was waiting, with red-rimmed eyes, to tell him that Ben had died. The news sent him racing out the back door to where the dog lay, covered with an old croker sack. Dropping to his knees beside him, Daniel pulled the sack away. There came an automatic sick feeling, and pain from a place that felt empty already.

For a moment Daniel didn't seem to know what to do with himself. He couldn't believe that Ben was dead. Choking back his tears, he reached out and gently passed his hand over the lifeless body. He stroked Ben's fur, patted his head, rubbed his feltlike ears, picked up his paws; he touched his sleeping face. Slowly, it sank in that his old buddy was gone. Ben would never run out across the yard again to greet him, never again accompany him in their morning routine. Daniel pressed his palms against his eyes, trying to stop the tears. Over and over again in his mind, he said his name, *Ben, Ben, Ben...* Then, unable to fight it anymore, his grief overtook him and came forth in deep, anguished sobs.

Never having seen their father cry before, Rachel and Carson didn't know what to make of it now. It frightened them to see their big, strong daddy bawling like a baby. Rachel threw her arms around Amelia's waist, sniffling; Carson primped up to cry and hid his face in her skirts. Amelia took them by their hands and led them inside, calmly reassuring them that their daddy would be all right.

Daniel knelt beside Ben's body a few minutes longer. When he was in better control of himself, he went to the shed and got a shovel. He then went back and gathered Ben up as carefully as he could. Holding him close, he wept into his neck. With the dog in his arms, he walked, like an old man, carrying him to the woods to bury him, to say good-bye to him. Hard as it was, he knew it had to be done. He knew he had to do it—had to. Deaf to the sounds around him and blinded by the tears still pouring down his cheeks, with every few steps he wiped his face and nose on his shirtsleeve.

It was well after dark by the time Daniel returned to the house. He didn't act upset anymore, he was just quiet. It was a much stiller scene around the supper table than usual. No one said much of anything during the meal. Amelia had told Rachel and Carson it would be best for now not to say anything about Ben, and no one did. Amelia was a good cook, and the food was delicious, but Daniel had to force himself to eat. When Amelia handed him his coffee, his eyes met hers, and he smiled a little smile, but she saw the sadness behind the effort. He was crushed to the bone, she knew. But she understood. Daniel had raised Ben from a puppy. It could be said that the two of them had grown up together. Ben had been part of the family, a part of their lives, and they were all going to miss him terribly.

Daniel went to bed early, right after the children, only to lay thinking. When Amelia came to bed, he lay still, not wanting to talk as they ordinarily would. Tonight, he just didn't feel like it. After what had happened, he had not even felt like telling her about what it was like at Mrs. Adam's house and what a fine person she was, or about the cupboard he had for her. He had, at least, thought to give Rachel and Carson their toys. He'd surprise Amelia with the cupboard tomorrow, he told himself. Tomorrow he would feel better, and tomorrow he would tell her everything. He just didn't feel like talking tonight. Tonight, he just needed to be alone in his mind, alone in his misery, to think, remember, to clear his head.

As he lay there in the dark, Daniel tried to tell himself it was stupid to grieve so over a dog, that Ben couldn't live forever, but as the weight of his sorrow bore down on him again, he couldn't stop his eyes from welling up. He'd loved that old dog in a way that some could never understand, in a way he couldn't explain. He didn't know why. Although he made very little sound, he wept so hard the bed shook as if he had a chill.

Beside him, Amelia's face too was wet with tears, her heart breaking for Daniel. It seemed, though young as they were, together they had already endured enough heartache for two lifetimes. And enough joy. They had loved each other so deeply, for so long, sometimes she thought no other two people in the world had ever loved like they did. That's how she knew. Aside from his distress over Ben dying, she had a sense that Daniel was struggling with something else. For a few weeks now, she had felt as though he was hiding something. Or hiding *from* something. She couldn't imagine what it could be though. *Something.* But until he was ready to talk about it, there was really nothing she could do except let him know that she was there for him.

Without a word, Amelia moved over in the bed and put her arms around Daniel consolingly; Daniel put his arm around her and pulled her against him. The warmth of their embrace more comforting than a quilt, they held each other close and wept, until they were exhausted of tears and sank into sleep.

November 1863, the first Sunday

This morning at church we were told that just a few miles away, over in the next county at a place called Salsbattery, a band of Confederate deserters (outlaws) have organized and formed what they're calling the "Free State of Jones". Their leader is a man by the name of Newt Knight, and they are hiding out in the swamps and caves along the Leaf River. We've been warned that these outliers are a wild bunch of desperate, ruthless hooligans—making raids on small, poor farms like ours, stealing everything they can get their hands on, particularly guns, horses, and food. They're just as likely to kill us as not. Up 'til now, things had been relatively quiet here in Collinsville—we'd only heard rumors of such happenings far-off—and carried out by the enemy. This, however, brings it home—right up to our backdoors. I do wonder, what is to become of us all?

At this point, things are looking mighty bleak for the South. Grant seized Vicksburg back in the summer—

forcing our army to yield to the Union. (Our men did manage to hold out against the devils for more than forty days). Ironically, the surrender came on July 4, our great land's Independence Day. It's said that Vicksburg reeks of the thousands lying dead in the insufferable heat. Gettysburg was defeated the day before, our state capital, Jackson, was captured back in May. Last I heard, Luke's brigade had gone northward, toward Canton.

What news we get is slow in coming—obviously—and depressing, but as it comes through, articles about the war and lists of the dead and wounded are tacked up on the board at the post office. Ever' few days, Rachel and me walk to town, sick with dread, to look at it. It's hard to do, but impossible not to.

Even though the days grow ever shorter due to the time of year, to me each one seems longer than the last, like refrains to a depressing piece of music, relentless and harrowing, with nothing giving promise to an end to this dispiriting war-song. My spirit is weary—very, very weary today. Could I say, I would say, "Let it be over." I would say, "Luke, come home! Wherever you are, just walk away and come home!" How I pray that God will spare him.

A right smart came to church today. Old Brother Ishee preached a fine sermon.

CHAPTER 15

Children's children are the crown of old men...

*—Proverbs 17:6 (*KJV*)*

*B*eyond the fields of the Quinn farm, the Leaf River curved through cypress swamps and lowlands, past clay bluffs and pristine sandbars, coursing its way toward the distant gulf.

Since moving from town to the farm, Ellis had become his grandfather's constant companion. The two spent much of every day together, the boy following Ezra as closely as his shadow. Not that it ever mattered what they did, but today, they had gone fishing on the river.

The spot Ezra chose was in the shade, with the bank sloping down to the water. As soon as they arrived, Ellis spied a white crane standing in the shallows across the river and upstream aways. While Ezra rigged up their poles, Ellis found a rock, and rearing back in an aiming stance, he threw it as hard as he could at the crane. Despite his earnest effort, the rock went through the air only a short distance before dropping into the depths of the current. The bird remained statuelike, seemingly oblivious to the human intrusion.

Kneeling, Ezra baited the hooks with rooster liver and handed Ellis his pole. With a nod toward the water, he said in a voice hardly above a whisper, "Bet dey's a channel cat long as yo' arm lyin' up under dat snag yonder." Careful so the boy wouldn't get tangled up in the overhead foliage, he lent a hand as Ellis swung his line in an arc and let it drop just to the side of the submerged log. Ezra then dropped his own line and sat down on the bank beside his grandson.

As they fished, Ezra studied the water. He had a healthy respect for the river, knowing that it could take a man's life in the shake of a goat's tail. He couldn't swim; neither could his grandson. He let his eyes travel farther downstream to a place where a large soapstone formation jutted out over the stream, slowing the current and forcing the river to bend and slightly change course. The water there was deep and still, but from where Ezra sat, he could see the occasional swirl and eddy of a hidden whirlpool. The Leaf was a master of illusion—treacherous and tricky; Ezra knew its power lay just beneath its surface.

He looked up through the branches to blue sky; except for the faintest marbling of white, there wasn't a cloud to be seen. The air carried the fragrance of sweet earth and pine. Giving in to indolence, Ezra took a deep breath and closed his eyes for an instant, listening. The humming-chirping sound of the woods was so relaxing it could have put him to sleep.

"Wake up, Pawpaw. Dem fish see you 'sleep, dey gone sneak up an' steal yo' bait." Ellis grinned up at him and started giggling, and kept on giggling until Ezra laughed too. The boy's strongest love was for his Pawpaw Ezra.

Feeling a strong tide of tenderness for the boy, Ezra reached over and pulled him close; the boy brushed a bothersome gnat from his face. Thus they sat for a long while, boy and man, contented, watching their poles.

Suddenly, the end of Ellis's pole bent, and quick as an old man could, Ezra was up on one knee with the line in his hands. Together they pulled a good-sized catfish onto the bank, it fighting them with all it had. Ezra unhooked it, careful of its spiny fins.

"Yassuh, dat a nice 'un," he said. "Come suppertime, we gone see how dis ol' cat daddy look swimmin' round in a pan o' grease." He made a little sound and licked his lips.

Ellis examined the fish proudly for a minute. Then he said, "Let's go home an' show him to Granny." He'd had enough fishing for one day.

Ezra pulled his own line in and noticed that most of the liver had been nibbled off the hook. He gathered up their poles and the fish and started slowly up the bank, losing his balance, slipping a time or two as he climbed. Ellis toted the bait, skipping along barefoot, graceful and energetic as a deer. As if on cue, the white crane finally lifted itself from the river and soared up and away, disappearing into the woods.

A half hour later, Ezra and Ellis were sitting on the back doorstep, eating, their plates loaded with cold peas and cornbread, pickled okra, and thick slices of onion, because their overalls were too dirty to eat in the kitchen. Besides that, they were men, and everyone knew that kitchens were for girls.

CHAPTER 16

Vanity of vanities, saith the preacher; all is vanity.

*—Ecclesiastes 12:8 (*KJV*)*

*S*arah Beth Warren had hated growing up in the country and had taken to living in Memphis with a flourish. Now twenty, at sixteen she had eloped with Abigail's brother, Jonathan Langston, whereupon she'd enthusiastically set about spending his money, at last having come into, in her eyes, a role befitting her.

It was the late, elder Langston who had founded the family's bank, and attributive to his shrewd business sense, he had managed to avoid financial ruin despite the revenue collapse and loss of Memphis's charter during the latter part of the century; wherefore upon his death, Jonathan and Abigail had inherited a vast estate. Like his father, Jonathan knew much about investment strategies and operating the bank; he applied himself earnestly to his work, frequently staying at the bank until after supper, sometimes even late into the night.

To say Jonathan and Sarah Beth loved each other would be an exaggeration, at least to say there was any *true* love between them. Sarah Beth was purely vain and wholly selfish. She loved only herself. Jonathan did, though, love his young wife's liveliness and energy; her wit and spontaneity amused him. They lived in a stylish townhouse near the waterfront—managed efficiently by a housekeeper, a cook, and a man named Dicey, who served as both their driver and gardener. They were a handsome couple; they seldom disagreed, they attended important functions together, they danced well together. Sarah Beth had a flair for hosting memorable dinner parties; she turned a blind eye to Jonathan's infidelities, and he paid no attention to her extravagant spending. One might say theirs was a happy arrangement.

Since eloping with Jonathan, Sarah Beth had gone back to Oakdale only once to visit her family, and that had been almost two years ago, for Christmas. She wrote to them more frequently, usually once a month if the spirit moved her, and usually when she wanted to boast about something new she had purchased. Quintessentially shallow, she once held a dinner party for the sole purpose of showing off a costly Aubusson rug, only to secretly begrudge those who walked on it, for in doing so, in her mind, they had defiled it, and made it common.

Travis had replied to Addie's letter promptly, and within a matter of days arrangements had been made for Asher and Penelope to travel to Memphis so Libby could be seen by Dr. Alexander. Thrilled at the prospect of visiting her daughter, Laura decided to accompany them on the trip and stay the week with Sarah Beth.

On the day they were to arrive, Sarah Beth found Jonathan at his usual place at the dining room table, reading the newspaper as he ate breakfast. "Good morning, my darling," she said. She went quickly to the sideboard, first taking a moment to gaze at her reflection in the gilded mirror that hung above it, marveling at the perfection of her complexion and fluffing out her hair before serving herself from the delectable array of meat and pastries the cook had prepared.

"Good morning," Jonathan said absently, sipping his coffee. "Did you sleep well?"

"Tolerable," she replied as she slipped into her chair.

His eyes still on his paper, Jonathan murmured, "I trust you're excited that your mother is coming on the train this afternoon. And your uncle and aunt, and cousin."

Without really answering him, Sarah Beth replied, "I still can't believe it's taken them this long to realize what I could have told them all along. That nutty little creature – Libby – was always doing something crazy." She spooned sugar into her coffee and stirred it. "How well I remember, I was sitting on the porch one day, churning…I actually *saw* her stomp an anthill, then stand on it barefoot—just stood there, mind you, not batting an eye while a thousand ants stung the fire out of her! Just imagine it, if you can– " She buttered her toast and bit into it, talking as she ate, "*Me*, of all people! *Churning*! Law! What a loathsome task that was! Am I ever so glad those days are over and done with!"

Jonathan lowered his newspaper and glanced over at her as she babbled on.

"And I assure you"—she had to stop and laugh—"that nut didn't fall far from the tree! Everybody in Oakdale knew Aunt Anna was a fruitcake! Oh yes, it was the talk of the town, the way she drowned herself." Rolling her eyes, she reached for the society column of the paper. "Please, Lord, don't let me start remembering things, or I'll get the williwaws." For a moment, she peered at the newspaper. She turned a page. "Hard to imagine Uncle Asher would dare marry again, having tried it first with her." She said it aloud, but to herself, then shook her head, dismissing the idea. It was too early in the morning to be pondering the senseless motives of morons and idiots. She was just thankful she no longer lived in that backwoods bedlam. Stuck out in the middle of nowhere, miles from town—not that anything exciting ever happened in

Oakdale—all her family did was work, sunup to sundown, with little to show for it, and then went to church on Sunday. What a trifling life! It was beyond her how anyone could seemingly be so content with such a dreary existence. She had suffered through it for sixteen long years, but never again! Meeting Jonathan was the luckiest thing that ever happened to her. He had given her an escape from that life; eloping with him was like breaking out of prison. *Money*, she thought. *Life is so much better with money.*

Sarah Beth had her legs crossed and was swinging a foot in a way she sometimes did. From behind his paper, Jonathan watched her for a moment. Sometimes when he looked at her, beyond prettiness, *and reckless spending*, he saw nothing. This was one of those times. *Does she never consider anyone but herself?* he wondered. He knew she was not proud of where she came from. In fact, as he thought about it honestly, he knew she felt her family was not good enough for her. He, however, could give her no support in her feelings; he saw the Warrens as good, decent people. They bore no grudge to him after he and Sarah Beth eloped. If anything, he was quite taken with their friendliness and how they welcomed him as their son-in-law when they had gone back among them for Christmas. Sometimes he feared himself a fool for marrying her. There were times he wished he had listened to Abigail. She had tried to warn him. He was now thirty-six years old. Of late, he had found himself wondering, *What will we find to talk about once…*

He stopped himself abruptly from that line of thought. It was too depressing.

Feeling genuine concern, he said, "Sad for the poor girl. She must be terribly bad off if they're bringing her all this way to be seen by a psychiatrist. Maybe she will find the help she needs up here." He watched as Sarah Beth stuffed the last of her toast into her mouth, and when she didn't reply, he said, "Still again, I'm sure you're looking forward to showing your mother around the city?" It was a question this time.

Sarah Beth managed an "mm" while she finished chewing and swallowing. "I suppose it'll be fun." Her eyes mocked him briefly. "However, I can't imagine it'll be fun for either of us, having to wear our church manners for a whole week." She said it half-kidding, but Jonathan knew she was serious.

Forcing himself to smile, he stood up and gave Sarah Beth a husbandly peck on the cheek. "If I'm to make it home in time for dinner tonight, I must go to work."

He left then, and Sarah Beth went to find the cook to discuss the menu.

At three o'clock, Travis drove the carriage to the train station; Dicey followed with a wagon. Asher, Penelope, and Libby were to be guests of Travis and Abigail; Laura would stay with Sarah Beth.

In good time the train arrived, and as soon as the weary travelers stepped down onto the platform, Travis called out a welcome. As Sarah Beth went toward her mother, she wondered, not for the first time, *How could she make such a mockery of style?* She found it irritating that she cared not a whit for pretty clothes. *I wouldn't be caught dead wearing that dress if I'd been stripped naked*, she thought.

"Sarah Beth!" Laura cried happily when she saw her. Laughing, she grabbed her daughter and held her tight. After a moment, she pulled back and looked into her face, beaming. "It's so good to see you! Let me look at you!" For a minute, she was slightly in awe of the beautiful young woman Sarah Beth had become. To her, she looked taller, and she was so poised. And she'd never seen such a tiny waist. For a second, she tried to imagine her with a ninth-month belly. She had secretly thought, rather hoped, that by now she and Jonathan would have made her a grandmother. "Oh my gracious, it's so *good* to see you!" she exclaimed, squeezing Sarah Beth's hands affectionately.

"It's wonderful to see you too, Mama," Sarah Beth replied.

"Oh, I'm awful!" Laura said, turning to Penelope, then back to Sarah Beth. "Sarah Beth, you remember Penelope?" To Penelope, she said, "Isn't my daughter just *beautiful?*"

Sarah Beth laughed, despite herself. "It's good to see you, Penelope, and you too, Libby." Libby smiled at her shyly.

Agreeing with Laura and noticing Sarah Beth's lovely complexion, Penelope asked, "How on earth do you stay so fair?"

Sarah Beth smiled and waved her hand lightly. "Why, if I didn't stay out of the sun, I suppose I'd be as speckled as a guinea too." If any noticed the slight, it didn't show. Especially Laura, so happy she was to see her daughter again.

While Dicey loaded their belongings onto the wagon, the others settled into the carriage, and Travis took the driver's seat, and off they went.

Deep into the night, Louella Stinson lay awake, lost in her dreams. After all, she had a whole new life to dream about now. Three weeks before, Wilkes had asked her—Little Miss Nobody—to marry him, and since, she had been too excited to think of anything else. In just two short weeks, she would become Mrs. Wilkes Graham, and he would become her husband, *and her benefactor.* A voice inside her was shouting for joy; it was the happiest time of her life.

In truth, she had almost been sorry about how it happened, *almost*, but then she realized it didn't really matter. Once they were married, they would be so happy together he would forget all about it, as would she.

On the night Wilkes proposed, they had been fighting. He had hit her, again. She had endured his abuse previously because of how much she loved him, but that night she decided not to take it anymore. She wouldn't throw herself on his mercy this time.

Not knowing if she would be making a mistake, she had taken a daring chance. Over the past months, she had spent a lot of sleepless nights thinking about it, about what might happen if she ever brought the subject up. She had known all along the information might someday be useful, that it could either save her or destroy her.

There had been an interminable silence. Louella had held her breath as she waited for his reaction. Knowing what he was capable of—that the man she loved was a murderer—she realized it was a very serious and deadly game she played with him.

But her gamble had paid off.

It was amazing, incredible, nothing short of a miracle, how things had turned out. Overnight, Wilkes had shown himself another man. Never had anyone been more loving and kind and thoughtful. If he felt he was being manipulated into marriage, he gave no sign of it. He was spending more time with her now; he talked to her about how tobacco was grown, and he sat in the kitchen and kept her company while she cooked. Once or twice, he had even helped her with the dishes. That very evening they had sat outside on the porch together, gazing at the moon and stars.

Everyone makes mistakes, Louella told herself. To protect herself, and to ensure her own future, she was willing to forget everything in the past. *Forgiving each other for our past sins will only make our marriage stronger.* As far as she was concerned, whatever had happened down in Mississippi was finished. That was years ago; what was done was done. Most importantly, she had come out smelling like a rose.

Had Louella gone outside and looked before she drifted off to sleep, she would have seen that a curtain of storm clouds had gathered, and erased the moon and stars from the sky.

CHAPTER 17

The Lord is on my side; I will not fear; what can man do unto me?

—Psalms 118:6 (KJV)

At ten o'clock the following morning Dr. Alexander's receptionist escorted Asher, Penelope, and Libby into his office, then went out, closing the door quietly behind her. Rising to his feet, Dr. Alexander introduced himself, shaking hands with Asher. He looked at Libby and smiled.

"Mr. and Mrs. Bradley, Libby, I've been looking forward to meeting you all." Libby was eyeing him suspiciously. "Please, sit down." To Asher and Penelope, he asked, "Would either of you like a cup of coffee?"

"Thank you, no," they replied. They found his manner very reassuring.

He sat, asking, "Libby, was yesterday your first time to ride a train?"

Libby nodded, saying nothing.

"Sometimes I don't feel like talking either," he said, trying to put her at ease.

Looking at Libby, he saw a slight child, much more petite than he had imagined she would be; her hair was very blond, almost white as cotton. There was a devastating sadness in the solemn, blue eyes that stared back at him. *Here is a teenager so disturbed that she drowned a defenseless puppy in a creek.* There was an explanation for everything, he knew, and he was very eager to start their sessions, to find out what was going on behind that intense, blue stare.

Addressing all three of them, he said, "As you know, I've spoken to Travis." He paused. "It's my understanding, Libby, that you've been having bad headaches for some time now. This, no doubt, causes you much distress, and of course, causes your parents great concern. There is a reason that you're having these headaches – something is causing them – and this is why they've brought you here to see me, in hopes that I can help you." After another brief pause, he said, "Travis told me what happened to your mother. I'm sorry." Libby was looking at him, her eyes now filled with tears. "I would like to try to help you, Libby. Will you let me try?" He could tell she was wary of him.

Libby glanced at her father uncertainly. Asher smiled at her reassuringly and said, "It's all right." Finally, she looked back at Dr. Alexander and nodded.

"Excellent!" Dr. Alexander exclaimed. He got up and walked around his desk. "To begin with, a nurse is going to take you downstairs for a brief physical examination. In the meantime, I'll be speaking with your parents, making some notes about your medical history." He opened the door and summoned his nurse. "Nurse Porter."

A nurse in a starched, white uniform came in and took charge of Libby, leading her from the office.

That afternoon Libby met with Dr. Alexander again. This time they were alone, except for his nurse.

"Did you have a good lunch?" he asked her cheerfully.

"Yes, sir," Libby answered timidly.

"Good." Dr. Alexander opened the folder lying before him on the desk. "Well, after speaking with your parents this morning and now having reviewed your bodily assessment, I see no apparent *physical* reason that would cause you to experience the sort of reoccurring headaches you suffer from." After a brief pause, he said, "You are aware, are you not, that I am a psychiatrist, that I treat problems of the mind?"

Libby nodded. "Yes, sir."

"As I explained to your parents this morning, Libby, one's mind is a very delicate thing, but also very adaptable to certain situations. It is designed to cope with only a certain amount of pain, and when it can stand no more, it sometimes hides things in an attempt to protect itself from being hurt even more." He was trying to explain it on a level she could understand.

"My feeling, Libby, is that some bad things have happened to you. I think you've been badly hurt, and I think you're angry or afraid of something, or of someone. I think you're keeping all that anger and hurt and fear bottled up inside, so much that it builds up, and finally explodes inside your head, causing you pain of a different sort. I think that's the reason for your terrible headaches."

Dr. Alexander saw that tears were gathering in Libby's eyes. Deliberately ignoring them, he said firmly, "I really want to help you, Libby, and I believe I can, but that will depend largely upon you—and your willingness to trust me. In order for me to help you, you are going to have to be completely honest with me. Do you understand?"

All of a sudden, Libby burst into a fit of crying. Dr. Alexander sat quietly, watching her, letting her cry herself out. *Poor child*, he thought. It had no doubt been traumatic for her to lose her mother at such a young age. That in itself was one of the most tragic events that could befall any child. That her mother's death was self-inflicted made it doubly tragic. Yet still, his gut told him there was something far worse sequestered deep inside this girl's psyche, and if this were true, he wanted to draw it out and make her face it so that she might have a chance of becoming a happy, normal person. He didn't like seeing her cry, but he knew if he were going to have any success in treating her, he could not show her pity.

When the sobbing subsided and Libby gained control of herself, he gave her a handkerchief and said, "There now, that's better. Would you like a glass of water?"

Libby shook her head no. With trembling hands, she blew her nose.

Dr. Alexander leaned forward. Speaking in a gentle, reassuring tone, he asked, "Are you afraid, Libby?"

Libby hesitated, staring at him. She answered softly, "Yes."

He said, "Then let us, you and I together, face your fears so you can stop being afraid."

Just then, there came a soft knock on the door. Dr. Alexander looked at his watch, surprised to see that an hour had passed already. It was time for his next appointment. He regretted not having more time to spend with Libby, but felt as though they had at least established an understanding. He knew she did not yet feel completely comfortable with him—that would have been too much to expect—but she did show a willingness to try and a desire to be helped. To his experience, it was a productive first day. Besides that, he knew the Lord was on their side.

With an apologetic smile, he said, "I have another patient to see now. You and I will pick up here in the morning." As he watched her walk out with the nurse, he sat at his desk wondering, *What is it, Libby, that you are so afraid of?*

He was anxious to find out.

The following morning at nine o'clock, Dr. Alexander's receptionist announced, "Libby Bradley is here, Doctor."

"Send her in," he replied.

Libby walked into his office slowly.

Dr. Alexander smiled and said, "Good morning. It's good to see you again, Libby. Come, sit down."

Libby sat down across from him. Today, her hair was plaited and stylishly wound around her head, which made her appear a bit more mature than she had looked the day before.

"Is there anything you would like to tell me this morning?" Dr. Alexander asked.

The question threw Libby completely off guard. She didn't know what to say, so she said nothing.

Aware that his time with her was limited, Dr. Alexander said, "Let's get right down to business then, shall we?" He leaned forward in his chair. "Yesterday we were discussing fear and anger, and how I thought they could be the cause for your headaches. This morning, I'd like us to talk about one of the things you told your father." He looked into Libby's face. "You told him that you had seen your mother's ghost on a few occasions since her death. Can you tell me what you were doing, where you were, and when this occurred?"

Libby was sitting rigid in her chair. When she spoke, her voice was barely audible. "The first time she…came back…I was asleep, and woke up…it was dark…I saw the curtains move an'…when I rolled over, she was standin' beside my bed…watchin' me." She remembered that she was wearing a long, flowing dress.

"Are you sure you were awake? Is it possible that you could have been dreaming?"

"No. I was awake."

"Were you afraid?"

"Yes."

"Why were you afraid?"

Libby hesitated. "Because...because she was dead. She was a...ghost."

"You're saying the reason you were afraid of her was because she was a ghost?" Dr. Alexander's voice was patient.

Libby nodded. "Yes."

"All right. Tell me about the next time you saw her."

Libby thought for a minute. "I can't remember exactly... sometimes she was there...but I couldn't see her."

"What do you mean?"

"Sometimes, I could...just...*feel* her."

"You mean like in your heart or in your mind?"

"No. Not like that. I could feel *her*...close to me."

"You felt her presence?"

Libby made a small nod. "Yes."

"How do you know you didn't just imagine it?"

Libby looked at the floor. "Well, because it seemed...real." And yet, there was a feeling of unreality about it too.

There was a silence. "Is there another time you remember seeing her?"

Libby took a deep breath. "I saw her in the woods one day... at the creek...I remember I heard breathing...in the trees...and then she...Mama...appeared."

"Were you afraid?"

"At first...but that day was...different."

Dr. Alexander paused as he thought about the creek, *and the puppy.* "Different in what way?" he asked.

Libby blinked. "I...I don't know." It was all so hard to explain. A moment later, she said, "I-I was mad."

"So that day, you were more mad than afraid. Were you mad at your mother?"

"Yes."

"Do you remember why?"

Libby's voice broke. "Because she wouldn't leave me alone! I wanted her to just go away and leave me alone!"

Dr. Alexander looked at Libby for a long moment. He said, "Libby, I'm going to ask you a question, and I want you to really think about it before you answer: Do you believe ghosts are real?"

As Libby sat there, thinking, he watched her face, and when the answer finally came, he saw it. Realizing, her eyes met his, and she looked at him for a moment. "No," she said.

It was a defining moment for Dr. Alexander. In consideration of her response, he was convinced that Libby had the capability to discern between reality and fantasy. Consequently, now more than ever he was certain that her problems stemmed from something she repressed, as a means of avoiding it. He said, "Libby, the images you saw of your mother were real, but they were from memories you have of her, stored in your brain. And the fear you felt when you saw those images is normal. For example, it would be normal for anyone to feel afraid if they thought they saw a ghost." He smiled. "I myself would no doubt keel over."

A small smile flitted across Libby's features, and then it was gone, almost as quickly as it had come, but it did not go unnoticed.

Dr. Alexander continued, "*If* the anger you felt that day in the woods was toward your mother, though I'm not thoroughly convinced at this point that it was, it probably was not from you *wanting* your mother to leave you alone, but likely due to the fact that she *had* left you alone. Perhaps you even felt she had abandoned you." He leaned back in his chair. "You see, when we lose someone we love, we experience many different kinds of emotions—sadness, anxiety, anger, denial, depression—until finally the grief process is completed and the loss has been accepted." These were all valid points for him to make, but he held to the idea that Libby's fear and anger came from some other source, an unconscious source other than her mother, and that she had released her feelings on the puppy in an act of displacement. *One step at a time, Stephen*, he told himself. "Does this make sense to you, Libby?"

Libby nodded.

Satisfied that they had made significant progress for one day, and knowing that it was important not to push her too hard, Dr. Alexander said, "Well, now that we've established that there's no such thing as ghosts, tomorrow we're going to talk about your dreams and explore some of the thoughts you have in your sleep."

Wilkes looked at the clock. It was one-thirty in the morning. A few minutes before, he had woken with an urge to relieve himself and was now standing beside the bed, staring down at Louella, watching her while she slept.

If it were not for her, he would have had no worries. He lived in his family home, he was making a name for himself in the tobacco business, he had plenty of money. Until recently, he came and went as he pleased, did as he pleased. In the past, he had spent a good part of his time in Richmond, away from the farm, playing in high-stakes poker games and being entertained by prostitutes.

Yes, his life had been perfect until he brought Louella home with him.

Wilkes cursed himself for the hundredth time for his lapse in judgment. He had not the slightest idea what would possess him to make such a stupid mistake—except she'd been beautiful and insatiable, and he'd been terribly drunk. Having her around had been fun for a few days – he'd had every intention of sending her packing after that – but while he was working in the fields and in the curing barn, she had slyly settled in, wiled him by cooking his meals, washing his clothes, heating his bathwater, warming his bed. She had been totally attentive to him, catered to his every want and need, never pressing, never demanding.

Now, she had succeeded in making his life miserable.

He thought back to a night a few weeks before. Her stupidity had made something explode inside him. He had grabbed her hair and thrown her on the bed. He slapped her hard across the face, trying to knock some sense into her. He remembered the rage he felt. He'd wanted to kill her right then. But something she said stopped him. To save herself, she'd taken a huge risk. "Hit me again an' I'll go to the authorities an' tell them what I know," she'd said. As it turned out, one night he'd made a drunken, boastful admission, and she had stashed it. She referred to it as her ace in the hole. As he had stood there weighing the situation in his mind, she had told him, calculatingly, "Or we can get married an' I'll forget all about it."

Hell hath no fury like a woman scorned. Considering his plight, he realized then what he had to do. He had no choice, he was imprisoned to her, and she to him. He dared not let her leave now. So, he'd put his arms around her and kissed her, begged her forgiveness, and promised to marry her. Why not? He'd made only one small request: that they wait until after the tobacco plants were transplanted. That way, he had explained, he'd be free to take her on a proper honeymoon, someplace special. She had jumped up and down ecstatically.

Wilkes had no choice now but to plunge ahead with his plan. Actually, he had to admit he was getting excited. The momentous day was fast approaching. The migrant farmers camped out behind the curing barn would soon be leaving, *in only a couple of more weeks.*

Presently, as he stood there in the dark staring down at Louella, his eyes were completely devoid of expression. He had never felt such contempt for anyone, had never despised anyone so much in his entire life. Then, remembering, he told himself, *No, that ain't true.* He had hated another like her, another stupid whore. *Anna Bradley.* She was the one responsible for the pesky situation he was in now.

Louella was only a couple of feet away from him, totally unaware of his presence. He bent over her, moving his hands slowly toward her neck. He could almost imagine her cries of pain, the feel of her bones crunching beneath his fingers. There was no way he was going to be at this slut's mercy for the rest of his life. He would not be controlled by anyone, and she was the only one who could connect him to what had happened in Mississippi. There would never be a wedding, and he intended to make her pay dearly for trying to blackmail him. He was going to do her a favor, himself a favor, and society a favor, and kill her. She was not fit to live anyway, but with her dead, he would be in the clear.

Suddenly, Wilkes came to himself. He shook his head to clear it; the red film before his eyes slowly lifted. No, he would not be at her mercy for the rest of his life, but he would be at her mercy for the rest of hers. And fortunate for him, hers would soon be over. He just had to keep his temper under control, be patient, and stick to his plan. *Only a couple of more weeks.*

The thought filled him with an indescribable sense of anticipation.

CHAPTER 18

Heal me, O Lord, and I shall be healed...

*Jeremiah 17:14 (*KJV*)*

*D*r. Alexander looked up with a smile as Libby entered his office and sat down in the chair across from him. "How do you feel this morning?" he asked.

"Good, I guess," Libby replied.

"Good," he said. "Then let's get started. As I mentioned yesterday, I would like for us to talk about some of the dreams you've been having, or rather, the nightmares. Tell me what you remember."

Libby thought for a minute. "Well...sometimes I used to, but not anymore...dream about my mother an'...in the dream...she would be..." She stopped, growing obviously nervous and tense. Dr. Alexander was watching her intently.

"What would your mother be doing in the dream, Libby?"

Libby started to answer and then stopped. She took a trembling breath. "We would be in the creek an'...Mama would be tryin' to drown me. She would hold my head under the water...*everything was cold and dark, my lungs were bursting*...I would fight...an' kick...*because I knew if I stopped fighting I was going to die*...in the dream I was barefoot...my shoes were on the creek bank...*sitting side by side on a patch of moss*..." She started crying softly.

Dr. Alexander sat there studying her, giving her a moment to calm herself. "When you would have this particular nightmare, did you ever die in it?"

Libby shook her head. "No. I always woke up before I died." She would wake up gulping for air, soaked with perspiration.

"Before your mother died, did you ever think that she had thoughts of killing you?"

Libby gave him a quick, strange look. "No."

"Do you remember how you felt when you would wake up from this nightmare?"

Libby thought. "I would feel...confused."

Dr. Alexander leaned back in his chair. That was not the response he expected. "Confused in what way?" he asked.

"I- I don't know...sort of like I couldn't remember if I'd had a dream or not, I guess." *But of course it was a dream...it had to be a dream.*

"But you haven't had that dream in a while. Is that correct?"

"Yes."

"What other things do you dream about that are disturbing to you?"

Libby hesitated. She knew what she was about to tell him was very important, because she knew it was the thing that caused her head to hurt. It was the thing she had not told her daddy. "Sometimes," she started, "I dream about a man...a mean, mean man." Her throat felt dry and scratchy; she needed a drink of water.

Dr. Alexander felt his pulse quicken. He looked over at Nurse Porter, who was keeping notes of the session. "In the dream you have about the mean man, Libby, what happens?"

Libby's heart started beating faster. "He...chases me."

"In your dream the man chases you?"

Libby saw how he was watching her. She nodded. "Yes." Then she shook her head no. All of a sudden she felt cornered; suddenly her face was filled with distress. "I dream about him *because* he chases me! He chases me in the woods! But don't tell Daddy, it'll only upset him!" As soon as the words left her mouth, she immediately burst into tears.

So he had been correct. Dr. Alexander could hardly believe it. He realized he was getting his first glimpse into Libby's secret world. "The man that chases you in the woods, Libby...do you know who is he?"

"No," she cried. "I – I've never seen him."

She has repressed his identity, Dr. Alexander told himself. But why? The aim of his therapy was to identify the source of her problem and bring it—whatever *it* was—back to the conscious level where it could be dealt with, and he felt he was on the verge of a significant breakthrough. Afraid that she might slam the door shut completely, he chose his words carefully. "Has the man in the woods ever spoken to you, Libby?"

"No," she replied. Her voice was shaky.

"Is he the reason you are afraid?"

Libby felt helplessly confused. She wanted to tell him what he needed to know in order for him to help her, but she didn't have the right answers. "Yes...but..."

He looked at her squarely. "Libby, I realize this is difficult for you to talk about, but has the man in the woods ever touched you or hurt you in any way?"

"No!" she screamed. "I told you I've never seen him when he chases me! Aren't you listening to what I'm sayin'? Why can't you understand me?" As she burst into racking sobs, Dr. Alexander rose and started around his desk to walk over to her, to try and calm her. In that moment, a flash of white light exploded in Libby's head and she saw a pair of sinister hands start reaching for her. She felt a pounding at her temples and knew she was going to have one of her headaches.

As Dr. Alexander moved toward her, she flinched. "Leave me alone!" she screamed hysterically. "Leave us alone!" She could not get the image of those hands out of her mind.

Hearing her screams from the hallway, Asher burst into the office. At a glance, he could tell that Libby was on the edge of panic. With an accusing look at Dr. Alexander, he yelled, "What did you do to her?"

Libby flew into his arms, crying, "Please, Daddy, please...take me home." Her head was throbbing violently. She just wanted to leave there, run away, *escape...*

Dr. Alexander saw the anger in Asher's face. Trying to reassure him, he said, "I'm sorry. It isn't always easy to talk about our problems, but I feel as though Libby and I are making excellent progress."

Asher retorted, "If this is your idea of excellent progress, we're done here. I'm takin' my daughter home!"

As Dr. Alexander watched them leave his office, he trusted when the man calmed down he would see things more rationally and allow him to resume his therapy with Libby. Then, thinking aloud, he said, "I suppose this would have been a bad time to approach him about using hypnosis on his daughter." While Nurse Porter suppressed a smile, he took a pad from his desk drawer and wrote out a prescription for Libby's headache. Handing it to her, he said, "See to it, please, that this is filled and delivered to Dr. Travis Hughes's residence."

"Yes, Doctor."

When the nurse went out, he sat there for a long while wondering, *Who is the man?* Whoever he was, he felt certain that he was the root of Libby's problems.

CHAPTER 19

The wisdom of the prudent is to understand His way; but the folly of fools is deceit.

—*Proverbs 14:8* (KJV)

*L*aura was fascinated by Memphis. There was so much to take in, it was almost overwhelming. There were modern brick buildings and dozens of shops on every street; on the corners men sold newspapers and magazines. A constant parade of people swarmed the sidewalks. There were women in stylish frocks carrying flirty parasols and city men in dandy attire, with heavy gold watch chains dangling from their waistcoats. Since their arrival, Sarah Beth had been their tour guide. They had lunched on Beale Street and taken strolls along the Mississippi River, resting on a stone bench to watch the boats and barges. They had watched artists paint, listened to musicians play and sing; once they stopped to watch a man perform tricks on a unicycle. How Laura wished Addie was there! She was going to have so much to tell her when she got home.

While they were waiting for their tea to be served, Laura edged her chair back, excusing herself. After a visit to the ladies' powder room, she made a slight detour so she might again pass through the spectacular lobby they had entered from the street. Yes, the lobby of the Peabody Hotel was indeed spectacular! She could hardly contain her excitement as she turned about slowly, admiring it all for a second time. Lively music filled the great hall, and there was a fountain surrounded by stands of Boston fern, the stands sashed with colorful silks and embellished with lavish bows. Bunting and flags draped the upper banisters. And there, at the top of the stairs—

That's when Laura caught sight of him. He was walking at a leisurely pace, not hurrying, dressed in a dark, tailored suit, which was his usual work attire. And just down the corridor, there was a woman, standing, *waiting*. And when the woman saw him, she smiled, not timidly, but slowly, softly, casually, *provocatively*. And he smiled too. The way she touched his arm…well, it was obvious there was no strangeness between them. They were comfortable with each other, old-shoe, the way couples come to be over time. Soon after, Jonathan, her son-in-law Jonathan, unlocked the door, and he and the woman disappeared into one of the rooms on the second floor.

For a moment, Laura couldn't move. She just stood there, her feet riveted to the floor, staring in shock and disbelief, feeling as though her heart had been crushed. There was no question in her mind what she'd seen. It was clear. In her heart of hearts, she knew that Jonathan was having an affair with that woman. But how could he? Why would he? Suddenly, she was overcome with a sense of sadness. All she could think of was Sarah Beth and the heartache she had coming to her. *Poor Sarah Beth!* Laura was filled with grief for her—and with anger for Jonathan. He had a complete lack of respect for Sarah Beth, consorting with that woman, in broad daylight, in a public place! He had not even tried to be discreet! She boiled inside, and for one insane moment, she thought about going up those stairs, banging on that door, and shaking him until his teeth rattled!

But the whole thing was so tawdry, so shameful, and embarrassing, all she really wanted was to get away from there, flee as far away from the scene as possible. She turned and blindly stumbled down the wide hall. Bumping into an elderly couple, she mumbled an apology. She didn't stop until she reached the powder room. There she bathed her face with a cool towel. Oh, Lord, what was she to do? Or was she trespassing on an area that was none of her concern, and should do nothing? But Sarah Beth deserved to know the truth. But the truth would ruin her marriage. She thought, *I've never known a single person who has gotten a divorce.* That sort of thing might happen here in a big town like Memphis, or maybe somewhere out in California, but never back home in their quiet, little community. Oh, what a mess! It seemed like an impossible situation.

Knowing that Sarah Beth and Penelope had no doubt begun to wonder what was taking her so long, Laura took a deep breath and straightened her shoulders. She could only hope that she looked composed enough to be convincing. Then feeling as withered as something that had been pressed in a Bible, she made her way back toward the tearoom.

It had taken Laura tremendous effort not to let her feelings show the remainder of the day. At supper, she managed to be civil to Jonathan, but not genial.

Yet unsure about what she was going to say to him, as soon as Sarah Beth went upstairs for her bedtime toilette, she marched purposefully into the library. Jonathan was at his desk, sitting in a high-back chair of rich leather that had been his father's. He glanced up when she came into the room, and closing the ledger before him, he stood, to beckon her.

"Come, sit. We've hardly had a chance to talk at all since you arrived. Tell me, did you have a nice time today?"

While he settled himself back in his chair, Laura moved toward him hesitantly, but did not sit down. Making an attempt to keep her temper in check, she replied, "No, we haven't really had a chance to talk. I never would have guessed the banking business required one to work such long hours."

Smiling, Jonathan replied, "It's the nature of the beast, I'm afraid."

His cheeriness irritated her, as did the fact that he showed no sign whatsoever of the momentous occurrence of the afternoon. Looking at him frankly, she said, "Really? Are you quite sure about that...because we went to the tearoom at the Peabody Hotel today for dessert, and I saw you..." She deliberately let her voice fade to silence. Then she continued, "Well, I'll just say it appears you like *your* sweets a little on the tart side." There was disappointment as well as sarcasm in her tone.

Jonathan's face went very still, almost stiff. He blushed awkwardly, but said nothing. After all, there was nothing he could say, really—nothing that his mother-in-law would understand anyway.

"I see," he then said carefully. He glanced her way but did not look *at* her.

Laura laughed shortly. "That's it? That's all you have to say for yourself? Sir, you are truly despicable!" She couldn't believe he made no attempt to explain or deny anything. Then again, the last thing she wanted to hear was a bunch of lame excuses and lies. There was nothing he could say that would change what she saw and *knew*.

Jonathan looked down at his hands, which he rubbed against his trouser legs, hesitating a long moment before saying, "I'm sorry, and I regret that you undoubtedly, and understandably, think harshly of me—"

"How could you do this to Sarah Beth!" Laura cried. "How could you destroy her happiness?" She couldn't help but wonder how long the affair had been going on, not that it really mattered.

"Mrs. Warren, I beg you…To begin, I urge you to ask Sarah Beth, and I'm sure your daughter will tell you that she is quite happy…"

"Of course I'm happy." Just at that moment, Sarah Beth glided into the room wearing a flowing, pink dressing gown. Looking from Jonathan to Laura uncertainly, she said, "What on earth is going on in here? From all the hubbub, you would think Granny Stell had rose from the grave."

Laura's eyes shot daggers at Jonathan, and just as he opened his mouth to say something, Sarah Beth interrupted, speaking to him directly. "Darling, do be a dear and leave Mama and me alone so we can girl-talk."

Jonathan rose from his chair gratefully, and with a short bow to Laura, he mumbled, "I bid you good night, ma'am." And he went out.

Once he was gone, Sarah Beth went over to the sofa near his desk and sat down, motioning for Laura to join her. "Dear Jonathan," she said musically, "he *is* the dearest and best husband in all the world, you know. Should there be any question, just look around."

Sitting down beside her, Laura took her daughter's hand and tried to find the right words. "Sarah Beth…I don't know how to say this. It hurts me to have to tell you, but I'm afraid you've been deceived." *In more ways than one*, she thought. "Today…at the Peabody Hotel…I saw Jonathan—"

Sarah Beth snatched her hand away and rose from the sofa abruptly. "Pray let's not talk any more about Jonathan, unless it's to say how wonderful he is or how much he adores me." Changing the subject, she asked, "Would you like anything from the kitchen? A glass of tea or milk perhaps?"

"He has a mistress!" Laura exclaimed. "He didn't even try to deny it!"

Sarah Beth shrugged. "So what if he does?" she replied indifferently. "She's nothing more but a passing folly."

Unbelievable! Laura looked horrified. Her voice faltered when she spoke. "Y- you mean you *know?*"

With a toss of her head, Sarah Beth said, "Really, Mama. Of course, I know. Jonathan's a *man*, for heaven's sake…if only you'd try, you'd understand that—"

Laura was beginning to lose her temper. "You really do beat all," she said.

"What?" Sarah Beth asked saucily.

"I should like *you* to understand something, young lady. Jonathan is making you look like a fool, and I'm starting to think you are one! For once in your life, girl, show some good sense! You don't have to put up with this!" Realizing her tongue was sharper than she had intended, she took a deep breath and said quietly, "Sarah Beth, you are my child, and I love you. You don't have to live a life of misery. You married so young, eloped, without really knowing Jonathan at all…"

Sarah Beth corrected her. "Again, Mama, I am not miserable." She loved her mother, but she was sick and tired of her trying to force her old, fogy ways of thinking onto her. She was not like her. She didn't see things the way she did. Sounding both accusing and defensive, she said, "You have always been so… good…and so…*proper*. I suppose it's your saving grace. But things are different now than in your day; things have changed."

Laura gave her a disputing look. "I don't know what *things* you are referring to, but certain things—like morals, values, and common decency—*never* change." *Jesus is the same yesterday and today and forever.* "And furthermore I'll have you know, God's code of conduct applies the same to both men and women." Sarah Beth's attitude was completely staggering to her. It was hard for her to conceive that she and Wesley had raised such an unprincipled, worldly child. She couldn't help but wonder where they had gone wrong with her. Thankfully, she thought, Wesley wasn't here to witness this. It would have devastated him.

Inwardly, Sarah Beth rolled her eyes and thought, *Spare me the sermon.* Having grown weary of the conversation, she said, "All I'm sayin', Mama, is that people are different. Some folks are content to live out their entire lives in cotton drawers, and if that suits them, that's fine by me. But as for me, I intend to poot through silk 'til my dyin' day." Then, pert and poised as a songbird, she went over and gave Laura a peck on the cheek. "I'm going up to bed now. So, sally forth, as they say, and night-night."

Laura watched sadly as her beautiful daughter mounted the stairs. She didn't know whether to laugh or cry. She loved her so much, yet, always hell bent on having her way, Sarah Beth had caused her more heartache than Jesse and Meggie put together. Still, it broke her heart to know how shallow and meaningless her life was. *Poor Sarah Beth,* she thought. She had always known the price of everything, yet the value of nothing. Now, here she was, married to a man she probably didn't give a whit for, who probably didn't love her the least bit either, except that he was wealthy, and she was content to pay the price for the lifestyle she'd grown accustomed to—the lifestyle she had always wanted. Difficult as it was for Laura to fathom the way they lived, she had to admit that Jonathan and Sarah Beth, for all intents and purposes, seemed to be a perfect match. *A match made on Fool's Hill,* she thought. *Oh, well,* she told herself, *I suppose that explains why I have no grandchildren.*

All of a sudden, for the second time that day, all Laura wanted was to be far away from there. She felt lonely. She missed Wesley. Looking toward the window, she wished more than anything that he would come riding up at that very moment—tall and straight, *faithful and true*—and take her *and* her cotton drawers home. *Home*—to their home-sweet-humble-home.

March 10, 1865

Our country has become a wasteland. Our "land of the free" is drenched in blood. This war has seen the capture and destruction of some of the South's grandest cities—Vicksburg, Nashville, New Orleans, Memphis; even Richmond and Atlanta have been burned to the ground. Our railways have been demolished, our fields are bare, our houses and barns are falling in, our livestock (what's left of it) is starving. Packs of deserters (from both sides), freed Negroes, and scavengers roam the countryside. I thought my brain would crack when we got word last week that Dalton had been hanged over in Cracker's Neck for stealing provisions from the Union Army. Once he fell in with that outfit over in Jones County, though, I guess it was just a matter of time before something like that happened. It's being said that the leader, the man Newt Knight, has forever ruined the good name of Jones County. He and his band of outlaws are considered such a disgrace to the Confederacy that folks have petitioned to change the names of both the county and the town of Ellisville.

To be honest, I fear I've grown numb to it all.

On a happier note, at least we haven't starved. This morning I killed a rabbit right outside the backdoor. That being the south side of the house, the grass is already up yea high, and I reckon he'd gorged himself all night long 'cause he was so fat he couldn't even outrun me. I knocked him in the head with a lightered knot—saved a shell. He was right tasty smothered in onions and gravy.

Not long after we ate, Rachel went into labor, and by the time dark fell, she had delivered a sweet, little baby girl. She is a pretty thing! Rachel named her Addie Virginia.

I guess that's proof that the miracle of life goes on, no matter how many men are dying every day.

Easter comes early this year; the dogwoods are in full
bud, azaleas too.

As Addie closed the journal, her heart ached over the words
Claire had written. She sounded so hopeless, so resolute. Addie
could almost feel her despair. What a sad and terrible time
that must have been. And to think, there were thousands upon
thousands of wives and mothers during that time who shared
those very same sentiments.

Addie wondered for a moment: Who was Dalton? And she
noticed there had been no mention in the journal that the men
had, at some point, been granted a furlough. Otherwise, she
would not have been conceived.

Letting her thoughts drift for a few minutes before she went
to bed, Addie found herself wondering about Libby. Hopefully
they would get an encouraging report from the psychiatrist Travis
arranged for her to see. And Laura, she could only image the fun
she must be having in Memphis! She could hardly wait for her to
come home so she could hear all about it.

CHAPTER 20

And ye shall know the truth, and the truth shall make you free.

—*John 8:32 (*KJV*)*

*I*t was early when Travis walked through Dr. Alexander's door carrying two cups of coffee. "Doctor, I'm afraid I'm a schizophrenic," he said.

Dr. Alexander was sitting at his desk, surrounded by papers and reports. Without looking up, he replied drily, "Well then, that makes four of us, and we're also paranoid. We lay awake all night wondering if we were the ones who are out to get us."

Travis had to laugh. Dr. Alexander looked up then, and grinned at him. They both had an endless supply of psychiatrist jokes, and demented senses of humor. They were constantly carrying on some kind of foolishness between them. Travis couldn't resist one more. "Why are you grinning at us like that?"

Dr. Alexander reached for his coffee. On a more serious note, he asked, "How is Libby this morning?"

Travis sat down. "I left before she got up, but her headache was gone by the time I got home last night." He gave his friend a tentative look. "Asher sent word by me that Libby won't be coming to her appointment today."

Dr. Alexander leaned back and let out a regretful sigh. "I was afraid of that."

"What happened yesterday, or would you rather not say?" Travis asked. He understood the rules of confidentiality.

"What happened is, we got real close to finding out what Libby's afraid of, then resistance happened. Other than that, I really can't say any more." There was a brief silence as Dr. Alexander looked toward the window. "Do you think there's any chance her daddy would consent to hypnosis?" If he could discover what Libby's mind was hiding, he could confront her with it so it could be looked at rationally and dealt with. Otherwise, he felt they were at a standstill.

Travis shook his head doubtfully. "I don't think he would ever agree to it."

"Do you think there's any chance he'll even let me talk to Libby again, or have I been ditched for good?"

Travis shrugged. "It's hard to say."

"Put in a good word for me, will you? I'd really like to help Libby, and I still believe I can. If only we had more time." Psychoanalysis was oftentimes a very long, slow process, sometimes taking years, and Libby would be going home to Mississippi soon. He said, "I might stop by your house this evening, see if I can patch things up with her daddy."

Travis nodded. "Is Miranda still in Chattanooga visiting her parents?"

"Uh-huh, she won't be home until Sunday."

"You're welcome to join us for supper."

"Thanks, it'll depend on what time I get out of here." He had enough work to keep him busy for a year.

Travis looked at his watch. Downing the last of his coffee, he got up to leave. "Well, time to go heal the sick. I have half a mind to go to that two o'clock meeting this afternoon," he jested.

When he got almost to the door, Dr. Alexander said, "Don't run with your scissors."

At five o'clock, as she always did, Nurse Porter stuck her head in to say good night. She was aware that some of the nurses she worked with had affairs with doctors, whether they were married or not, but hers and Dr. Alexander's relationship was strictly professional. He was one of the nicest men she had ever known, and he had always treated her with respect.

"I'll see you in the morning, Doctor," she said.

Dr. Alexander glanced up. "Good night, Nurse." As she turned to leave, he suddenly remembered and asked, "Hey, how's that little boy of yours doing?"

Her lips curved into a smile. "He's not so little anymore, I'm afraid. It's hard for me to believe he's already three." She sighed. "That boy worships his daddy. He imitates Jack's every word and deed. Well, try not to work too late."

"Good night."

A few minutes later, Dr. Alexander stood up and stretched. He was tired. He'd been at his desk most of the day. He'd gone over the transcript of his sessions with Libby several times, hoping to find some clue that might be of help. He knew that Libby was her own cure, and that the truth was imprisoned somewhere in her mind, but as her psychiatrist, he felt it was up to him to spring the trap so it could be released.

He walked over to the window and gazed out at the river, turning it over again in his mind. Everything he and Libby had talked about revolved around her mother's death. Yet she had not seemed overly emotional or distraught about it, which he supposed was appropriate given the time that had passed. She had not really become upset until she told him about the nightmare wherein her mother was trying to drown her.

As he stood there gazing across the river, something about that nagged at the corners of his mind. He went back to his desk and flipped to that page. He began reading it aloud to himself: "She would hold my head under the water...I would fight...an' kick...but I was barefoot...my shoes were on the creek bank."

It suddenly struck him as odd, completely implausible, that while caught up in the throes of such a terrifying situation someone would make such an inane observation. It didn't make any sense that someone fighting for their life would be concerned about where their shoes were. How was that relevant? He remembered during his initial meeting with Libby's parents how her father had mentioned that his wife's shoes were found on the creek bank when her body was discovered. Was this how Libby knew about the shoes? In the nightmare, was it her own shoes she saw, or...*were they her mother's shoes?*

Dr. Alexander's heart started beating wildly. Was it possible that Libby was there that night? that this was not just a nightmare but a piece of reality? Could she have witnessed her own mother's suicide? But in the nightmare, she was fighting, kicking. He suddenly thought about something Nurse Porter had said: her young son imitated his father's every word and deed. *He imitates his every word and deed—imitates, imitates.* And why had Libby said, "Leave *us* alone?"

And in that mind-smashing, heart-stopping moment, the pieces of the puzzle came crashing together and Dr. Alexander knew.

When Libby drowned the puppy in the creek, she was imitating something she had seen. And while her nightmares were real, the man who chased her in the woods was not; like Anna's ghost, he too was a memory. And whereas Dr. Alexander had initially thought the man to be a child molester, he now realized this was not true. For as the pieces of the puzzle tumbled into place, he realized the man was, in fact, a murderer. He knew that Anna Bradley had not docilely committed suicide – and he knew that Libby had witnessed and repressed the memory of her own mother's brutal murder!

Across town, as they all sat around the dinner table at Travis's house, they heard a loud knocking on the front door. A few moments later, without waiting to be announced, Dr. Alexander strode into the dining room abruptly. When Abigail saw it was him, she smiled and said, "Stephen, we had decided you weren't coming. We were just about to have dessert." She gestured for him to sit. "Please, sit down and join us."

Dr. Alexander hastily replied, "Please forgive me for barging in on you like this–" He paused for a moment, out of breath. He had run most of the way there from the hospital. Suddenly, everyone was staring at him.

"Are you all right, Stephen?" Travis asked with a look of concern. Dr. Alexander's hair was disheveled; his eyes were alive, verily glowing with excitement. He looked like a wild man standing there.

Ignoring the question, Dr. Alexander turned to Asher. "Mr. Bradley, I've come to ask your permission…Might I please speak to Libby—alone if possible? It's very important." Libby was staring at him, her eyes suddenly wide with apprehension.

Asher shook his head. "I don't think that's such a good idea, not after what happened yesterday."

"Please, I understand your reluctance…but it's crucial…there's something—" Dr. Alexander's tone was urgent.

"No," Asher said firmly.

But Dr. Alexander would not give up so easily. This was far too important. He had studied Libby's case from every angle, gone over all the potential scenarios in his mind, and he was absolutely convinced that he was right about what had happened.

With a step toward her, he said, "Libby, please…I want to help you, let me help you remember." It was only now really beginning to sink in to him how tormented she must have been all this time.

A surge of fear shot through her. "No! she shouted. She didn't want to remember. She was too afraid. "Daddy!"

Penelope reached over and placed a hand on her arm as Asher stood up and blocked Dr. Alexander's path. Now perturbed, he glared at him and said, "I'm warning you—don't upset my daughter!"

Seeing the look on Asher's face and puzzled by his friend's rudeness, Travis jumped up and hurried over to Dr. Alexander and grabbed his arm. "For God's sake, Stephen! That's enough! Get hold of yourself!" The way he was acting was completely out of character. Travis had never seen him lose control. "You're obviously tired; you've been working way too hard."

Realizing the seriousness of the situation, Abigail and Penelope sat there in astonishment, staring, saying nothing, waiting to witness whatever was forthcoming.

Dr. Alexander's mind raced frantically as he tried to decide what to do. He had a feeling that everything hinged on what happened in the next few minutes. He looked at Libby, knowing that this could be the turning point for her, the turning point to her health and happiness. It could change her whole life; it could set her free. Glancing at everyone apologetically, he said, "I'm sorry." Maybe they would forgive him for what he was about to do, but first and foremost, Libby was his patient, and he intended to do everything in his power to help her.

He turned again and looked at her. Libby met his gaze. Smiling at her reassuringly, he said, "I know what you're afraid of, Libby, and you don't have to be afraid anymore."

Libby stared at him uncomprehendingly as he went on, "I *know*, Libby. I know the truth about what happened that night. I know you were in the woods the night your mother died. I know what you saw…"

Libby sat there, suddenly filled with a terrible confusion. Everyone was staring at her, and then at him. Her eyes welled up with helpless, frustrated tears. She just wanted to be left alone.

Dr. Alexander's voice was gentle, hypnotic almost. "It's all right, Libby, you can tell us."

Libby started shaking her head. Why wouldn't he leave her alone?

"Tell your daddy, Libby; tell him what you saw."

Libby looked at her daddy and started crying. As Asher started toward her, Travis reached out a hand and stopped him gently.

Dr. Alexander said, "Everything's going to be fine, Libby… you're going to be fine. Just try to remember."

Subconsciously Libby knew that something awful had happened. She put her hands over her ears as if to shut it out. *What if it was too awful to know?* "Stop!" she pleaded desperately.

Dr. Alexander's mouth was dry. He swallowed and tried again. "I know you've been though a terrible ordeal, Libby. That's why you have the headaches. Tell your daddy about the man in the woods. Tell him what he did."

Asher looked at him, bewildered. "What man? What are you talkin' about?"

Dr. Alexander shook his head. With sober respect, he said, "It has to come from Libby." To Libby, he said, "Try to remember that night, Libby; try to remember what you saw." His voice was very soothing.

Libby took a deep breath and closed her eyes, and when she did, a floodgate opened over which she had no control. As images from the past began to surface in her mind, she felt almost disembodied. *She was walking along a path in the woods.* She seemed to know exactly where she was going. *She had gone down this path many times before.* There was an extraordinary energy about the place. Something had happened here, something terrible. *The trees were breathing…the woods were alive!* She heard frogs singing; she smelt the creek. *The night was so clear, so starry.* Her mother was there, sitting in the moonlight. *She was sifting sand through her fingers.* And there, on the creek bank, were her shoes, sitting side by side on a patch of moss. And there was something else too, someone else. *A man came out of the shadows and walked toward her...* Then something bad happened, something terribly, terribly bad...

Asher sprang at Dr. Alexander, grabbing him roughly by the lapels. In a booming voice, he said, "Confound you! If someone's hurting my daughter, I have a right to know! I demand you tell me!" His face was strained, his hands were trembling.

Dr. Alexander yanked free from Asher's grasp. Dubiously noting the man's clenched fists, he ventured stiffly, "As Libby's psychiatrist, I say again, we must let her remember for herself!"

A scuffle ensued, a chair was overturned. The women shrieked as Travis hastened to break the men apart.

In the fever of all the commotion, the air was split by a sound so loud and sharp it shocked everyone to silence. "It was *him!*" Libby cried. "*He* did it! He killed her! I saw Uncle Hiram's brother kill Mama!"

...like a bird from prison bars has flown...

It was shocking, of course, but after hearing Libby's story, there was no question in anyone's mind that Wilkes had killed Anna. The local authorities were notified, and at seven-thirty that evening, two investigators met and talked with Libby and Asher, with Dr. Alexander present. The investigators listened and took notes as Libby recounted in startling detail what she had witnessed that night, and when she told them that she had heard Anna tell Wilkes she was pregnant, they glanced at each other and nodded, a look of satisfaction on their faces. That provided them with a motive for murder, and in a murder case, it was imperative that two essential elements be proven: motive and opportunity. It seemed evident that Wilkes had killed Anna to cover up their secret love affair and to relieve himself of any responsibility for the unborn child.

The investigators then conferred with a judge and a special prosecutor, and the wheels of justice were set in motion. Since the crime was committed in Mississippi, therefore out of Tennessee's jurisdiction, a deputy was sent by rail to deliver a sealed, confidential report of Libby's testimony to Sherriff Wiggington in Oakdale. Upon reading the report, Sherriff Wiggington's mind immediately went back to a suspicious incident that had occurred three years before involving Wilkes and a man named John Rutland. Two days after a tornado had ripped through the community, he remembered, the Rutland man had come accusing Wilkes of stealing a roan gelding from him. He and the man had ridden out to Hiram's place to question Wilkes about the horse, but according to Hiram, his brother had left a few days before, headed back home to Virginia. It had been only a few days later, he recalled, that Algie Thomason discovered Anna Bradley's body floating in the creek. Believed to have been mentally distraught over losing her home in the storm, her death was ruled an unquestionable suicide. At the time, there had been no way of knowing, or any reason to suspect, that there was any connection between her and Wilkes.

Within an hour of receiving the information, Sherriff Wiggington set out for the county seat, where he met with the judge and the district attorney. From the report, all agreed that there did not appear to be any doubt that Wilkes Graham had cold-bloodedly drowned Anna Bradley in Cedar Creek. Warrants were promptly issued for his arrest and extradition.

Hiram would soon hear the grim news. After meeting with the judge and the district attorney, Sheriff Wiggington rode directly to the woodshop to tell Hiram what had transpired and to ask if he wanted to accompany him the following day to Virginia to apprehend Wilkes. As Hiram listened in silence, he could think of no useful reason for him to go, deciding that he would rather wait and visit Wilkes in jail upon his return to Oakdale, thinking to himself that sometime in the near future, probably after the trial, it would be necessary for him to go to Virginia to sign papers settling his parents' estate once and for all, including the house, curing barns, and property. Maybe Addie could go with him, he thought, and see his childhood stomping grounds.

There was no way for Hiram to say what he felt. He stood numb with sorrow and watched Sheriff Wiggington leave, then blindly turned, and went into the woodshop. There, he fell on his knees and wept bitterly, praying for his brother, grieving for him and for the life he'd taken, and for the life Wilkes had wasted. Their daddy had once said, "Seems like ever since Wilkes was big enough to sit in a saddle, he's been gallopin' t'ward the devil with his spurs dug in." What would their poor father say about this? Hiram wondered. Wilkes had always chosen a sinful path, and Hiram was thankful his parents didn't have to bear this, thankful they now lived in Paradise with the Savior, where there was no sorrow or sadness, no tears.

In the days to come as each would consider, question, ponder, and make peace with the situation, each in their own way, in their own time, Travis and Wesley would no doubt hear the echo of Hiram's own words: "*Wilkes always has been as rebellious as a patch of sawbriars...*" As for Asher, like everyone else, he was shaken and saddened to find out that Anna had been murdered, yet at the same time, there was some solace in knowing that she had not taken her own life. Her betrayal, he forgave easily, realizing that, and she, was part of his past life. Anna had been dead for four years, and as far as he was concerned, her failings had died with her. He loved Penelope now. Now, she and Libby were all that mattered to him.

Wilkes and Louella were sitting at the kitchen table eating supper when Wilkes stopped abruptly, halting his fork in midair and cocking his head to listen.

"What?" Louella asked.

"Thought I heard somethin'," Wilkes replied.

Then they heard footsteps crossing the porch and a knock on the back door. Wilkes studied the little flower print of Louella's dress for a moment, then, figuring it to be one of the workers, he got up to answer it.

When he opened the door, he found himself looking down the menacing barrel of a cocked pistol.

"Evenin'," Sheriff Wiggington said. "Remember me?" His voice was smooth and deep.

Louella gasped but did not move.

Though caught completely unaware, Wilkes steeled himself so hardly a flicker of surprise showed on his face. He was a cool one, rarely letting his face give away his inner thoughts. Staring into Sheriff Wiggington's eyes, he remarked casually, "Long way from home, ain't you, Sheriff?" A minute later, when two more burly, armed deputies showed themselves, he said, "An' I see you brought some friends with you."

Sheriff Wiggington was cool in a different way. "Yep, an' with them other three around on the front porch, you might say we've got enough to have ourselves a party," he said.

Wilkes stood stock-still, waiting, indecision etching his brow as he felt the trap closing slowly around him. Louella sat scarcely breathing, her wits blunted with confusion.

Keeping a safe distance, Sheriff Wiggington reached into his pocket and withdrew some papers. "This here's a warrant for your arrest. I'll be takin' you back to Mississippi where you'll stand trial, an' most likely hang, for the murder of Anna Bradley."

Wilkes's body tensed, but before he had an opportunity to react, the two deputies knocked him to the floor and bound his wrists with manacles. Suddenly, everything in him rebelled. Coming to his feet, he was like a man possessed. He lurched toward the table with a viscous snarl and cursed Louella. "Damn you, you deceivin' little slut! I should have killed you when I had the chance!" Before anyone could stop him, he kicked and broke a chair in a savage display of deadly strength.

With a cry of alarm, Louella cowered and raised her hands as if to shield herself from his searing wrath. "I swear it wasn't me!" she protested. "I ain't told a soul!"

It was several moments before they could subdue Wilkes and affix the restraints to his ankles. Sheriff Wiggington then told him, "She's tellin' the truth. An eyewitness came forward."

Wilkes said nothing.

After regarding him thoughtfully for a moment, Sheriff Wiggington asked, "I'm curious. Why did you do it? What drove you to kill that woman? Was it because she was carryin' your child?" He pressed, "Are you even the least bit sorry for killin' her?"

Wilkes laughed shortly. "Sorry? I don't even remember her."

There was something chilling in the way Wilkes said it that made Sheriff Wiggington pause. He sensed the cold, deadly untouchable core that was in him and knew that he was in the presence of evil, that somewhere along the way something in Wilkes had died, or had never been alive to start with.

His next words were directed at Louella. "What do you know of this, young lady?"

But Louella was deep in her own miserable thoughts. All at once, she had realized. It was over. Her dreams, her well-laid plans—over. The events of this night had ruined everything. Any hope she'd had of becoming Mrs. Wilkes Graham were ruined, any possibility of possessing his fortune, now ruined. The injustice of it was like a slap in the face. Why had everything gone wrong? Why now? Why did Wilkes have to kill that woman? Why had they waited to marry? Why—a three-letter word for misfortune.

"Answer me, miss. What do you know of Anna Bradley's murder?" Sheriff Wiggington repeated.

Louella blinked, coming back to the present. She was now looking at Wilkes with a coldness in her eyes. *It was you I loved and wanted to marry.* But her reply to the sheriff came meekly. "I- I only know what he told me...nothin' more."

The look Wilkes gave Louella was mocking, cruel, sadistic. Sheriff Wiggington said to her, "You'll have to come with us an' make a statement." And there was a possibility she would be charged with obstruction of justice.

As the deputies helped Wilkes to his feet and started leading him outside, he looked at Sheriff Wiggington and sneered. "You wasted a trip. Ain't no way you're takin' me back to Mississippi, an' ain't no way I'll ever stand trial for murder." *At least not for the murder of Anna Bradley...*

Wilkes was a man facing death. He had no illusions about his chances for acquittal, yet he had no intentions of dying in Mississippi. Just hours before his train was scheduled to depart, he demanded to speak with a lawyer, telling the warden that he wanted to make a deal. No one could imagine that he had anything to say that would change his fate, but that was not important. Every prisoner was entitled to legal counsel, so an attorney was summoned to his cell.

Two hours later, a deal had been struck, and the extradition order was void.

To the small group assembled in his chambers, the judge stated, "Gentlemen, let me make it clear that I do not doubt for a minute that the defendant Wilkes Graham is guilty of murdering Anna Bradley. However, it has been alleged by Mr. Graham that two other victims are buried somewhere on his property, those of his former business partner and his wife."

The revelation struck like a thunderbolt. Sheriff Wiggington stared at the judge in amazement, as every eye in the room did the same.

The judge continued, "For the families of Edward and Lucy Douglas, in exchange for a guilty plea for their murders and for leading authorities to the location of their graves, the defendant, Wilkes Graham, is remanded into the custody of the State of Virginia, and in accordance with the terms of his plea, this court does hereby waive the death penalty for these crimes."

Thirty minutes later, Sheriff Wiggington walked out of the courthouse into the freshness of the day. It was sunny and warm, and the beauty of spring was everywhere. Though he wanted Anna Bradley's murder avenged, he kept telling himself if Wilkes had been executed, his pain would have been over in a few minutes. This way, his punishment would last for the rest of his life, especially since he killed Edward and Lucy Douglas out of sheer and utter greed, because he was too money-hungry to share the profits of their tobacco business. This way, he lost everything—his wealth, his business, his freedom.

In that moment, as he stood on the steps of the courthouse in Richmond, Virginia, Sherriff Wiggington took a deep, cleansing breath, lifted his eyes to the blue sky, and let go of his contention. God had blessed him with a rich life. He and his wife lived peacefully, happily, thankfully. He was in good health, he was free to walk about God's green earth as he pleased, and he was going home today, to Mississippi.

What more could one ask than that?

By the time Dr. Alexander arrived at the train station Friday morning, the passengers were already boarding. Through the crowd and chatter, he spotted Libby standing on the platform with her family, the sun glinting off her white-blond hair. Travis was there, as was Abigail, and Jonathan and Sarah Beth. All of them were laughing, crying. Not wanting to intrude upon their farewells, he stood back.

As he stood there, he thought, how strange it was, everything that had come to pass in just one week. Looking at Libby, he could not help but marvel. *She led us to the truth.* Who would have ever dreamed that a poor, disturbed girl, living in shadow, would have the key to solving such a diabolical case locked away inside her mind? *Three murders.*

As he watched her, Libby happened to turn her eyes in his direction. Their gaze met, but he guessed that she felt shy, maybe uncertain, or uncomfortable, for she quickly looked away, seemingly not wanting him to approach her.

But then, in a few minutes, she turned loose of her daddy's hand and started toward him, hesitantly at first, then running, her eyes shining with tears. Without saying a word, she threw her arms around his waist and held on to him tightly. As he put an arm around her shoulders, Dr. Alexander felt a surge of emotion within him, half-joy, half-thankfulness for having been blessed with the opportunity and the ability to help this child. By and by, Libby pulled away from him, and they walked together, hand in hand, to the platform to join the others.

As the train pulled out of the station, Dr. Alexander did not wave. Under his breath, he simply whispered, *Go with God.* He knew he would never forget Libby Bradley. Maybe still a little different from the perceived norm, and the healing was not complete—he knew as much—yet still, she was going to be fine. At least she was no longer afraid.

Noting the time, he turned quickly then and walked away, with a smile on his lips, in the direction of the hospital.

CHAPTER 21

*Let a man so account of us, as of the ministers of Christ, and
stewards of the mysteries of God.*

—*1 Corinthians 4:1 (*KJV*)*

*N*ot fifty paces down the road from Hiram's woodshop, a
short back road, unmarked by a signpost but known as the
Double Branch Pass, angled off the main thoroughfare and ran
through a neck of hardwoods, pine, and cedar. Sparsely traveled,
except by members of the family, the one-lane clay and gravel
road came out at Daniel and Amelia's farmstead, although the
property was still commonly referred to by most everyone in the
county as the old Lewis Place, for its original owners. Walking,
not hurrying, it took no more than twenty minutes to get from
one end of Double Branch Pass to the other, so there was much
foot traffic back and forth, especially among the women and
children, between the Graham, Coulter, and Warren households.

It was near evening at the end of an uneventful workday as
Daniel started for home. He walked, thinking his own thoughts,

his thinking inevitably turning to wondering what Amelia might be fixing for supper. As he went along, he picked up a stick and whacked at some tall weeds growing down the center of the road. When a bright-red cardinal flew out of a patch of dewberry briars bordering the road, it made him think about how good a mess of quail would taste. Fried chicken would scratch his sweet spot just as well, though.

In time, he rounded a bend and came up on a stretch of road where several giant oaks stood in a long, straight line on either side of the narrow lane. The way their tops spread and came together blocking out the sunlight, it seemed very much like entering a dark corridor, especially in the summer when the trees were full-leafed. As he passed through it, Daniel looked up. Through the lacework of branches and foliage, only a few patches of blue sky were visible.

Emerging from the shadow of the trees, he heard something, a slight sound, like something moving in the dry brush behind him. He paused and turned around. There, not thirty feet away, making its way along the embankment, was a dog. Upon seeing Daniel stop, it stopped. It stood rooted to the ground, not moving a muscle, just blinking its big, brown eyes.

In that instant, a pang of the most awful kind stabbed Daniel, one of emptiness and regret. Just seeing the dog pressed a place in his heart not yet healed. It made him think of Ben; he still missed Ben, and probably always would.

He turned and resumed walking.

A minute later, though, he glanced back over his shoulder to look at the dog again, as though something compelled him to do so. The dog was still following him, tentatively. Daniel stopped in the road, and the dog stopped and pricked up his ears. When Daniel started toward him, the dog cowed down and whined. Not wanting to scare him off, Daniel knelt down in the road. "Hey there, you lost, ol' boy?" he said. The dog whined again. Daniel held out his hand. "Come here." Stretching his hind legs to their full length, the dog flattened himself on the ground. Crouching, he crawled forward a short distance and stopped. "Come on, don't be afraid…I'm not gonna hurt you," Daniel said in a reassuring tone. The dog came on again, cautiously, wagging his tail slowly, easing up to Daniel. Daniel reached out and touched the dog's head. He conceded that he was a good-looking dog, a black-and-tan hound, about half-grown. Other than a few burrs and dry mud in his coat, he seemed fine. Probably somebody's coon dog, Daniel thought. "Where'd you come from?" He took the dog's ears in both hands and scratched them; the dog put his head on Daniel's knee. "What's this?" Daniel asked. He had felt a tag on the dog's collar. Examining it, he read the name: *Jonah*. "Is that your name? Jonah? Or is that your master's name?" No one named Jonah came to mind. He ran his hand lightly over the dog's muzzle; the dog looked trustingly into Daniel's face.

Though he had vowed never again to love a dog the way he had loved Ben, Daniel had to admit, there was something about Jonah that pulled at him, something in his eyes that seemed to speak to his soul. Until he could find out who he belonged to, he felt obliged to take care of him. The very least he could do was feed him and give him a warm place to sleep. The dog looked tired and hungry. "You wanna to go home with me, Jonah… get somethin' to eat?" Daniel asked. The dog barked three times. Daniel looked at him with a broad smile. "I'll take that as a yes."

It was a beautiful day, and Daniel felt good. Jonah trotted alongside him as they went down the road, glancing up at him occasionally, as the two made their way home.

CHAPTER 22

Fear thou not, for I am with thee; be not dismayed, for I am thy God; I will strengthen thee, yea, I will help thee; yea, I will uphold thee with the right hand of my righteousness.

—Isaiah 41:10 (KJV)

*E*zra and Obie and Ellis sat around the table in the center of the kitchen eating breakfast. Although Sassie had nursed Star earlier, the baby would be fed from the table when she woke the second time, which ordinarily was around seven-thirty or eight.

Still in her housecoat and with a rag tied around her head, Rosette sat down with a cup of black coffee, which was all the breakfast she ever took. She watched Ezra fork a mound of buttery grits into his mouth, followed by a piece of dripping, fried egg; he used a biscuit to sop up the runny yolks on his plate. Shaking her head disapprovingly, she said, "I don't see how you do dat." She then went into a rambling monologue about how rich, greasy victuals first thing in the morning had always set hard on her belly and aggravated her gallbladder.

Ezra continued eating and remained silent.

After a slow sip of her coffee, Rosette set her cup onto the saucer on the table and said what she was thinking then. "Woke dis mawnin' wif mayhaw jelly on my mind." They had eaten all the jelly she'd made the year before; there was still several jars of pear and fig preserves in the cupboard, but no jelly. And Rosette was partial to jelly, especially mayhaw jelly.

"A big piece of jelly cake would sho taste good right about now." Rosette stared at Ezra, and then at Obie, waiting for a response. If they heard—and they did—they ignored her. So she continued, "If I didn't haf to look after deez chi'rens today, I'd go see if dey wuz any turnin' down by da back field." Not that she actually intended to go; her work seldom took her farther from the house than the wash area in the backyard. Yet still, it was the end of April, and mayhaws would be ready now, and she wanted to make some jelly.

Ezra swallowed and replied, "You need to let me an' Obie go see. Las' time I wuz back in dere, thangs had growed up a sight. Briars wuz waist high, hedge up over my head—'bout got los' myself. Saw a big hornet nest too." He shook his head. Thinking out loud, he said, "I reckon dat hateful ol' hedge gone take over da world." In his younger days, Ezra had taken pride in his land, always kept it cleared, but he had gotten old and tired. He no longer had the energy or the heart to keep fighting scrub. Marked by too many seasons of neglect, the back twenty acres he spoke of was, in his eyes, too far gone to trouble himself over anymore. It ran right along the bank of the river and had become a jungle of vines and briars, sassafras, hedge, joe-pye weed, and goldenrod.

Just then, Sassie stepped in from the back porch carrying a bucket, letting the door slam after her. "Milkin's done," she announced cheerily.

Rosette's automatic response was, "I sho hope you scraped yo' shoes befo' you came in, seein' how dey's been in dat nasty barn lot."

If it be possible, as much as lieth in you, live peaceably with all men. Sassie said the verse to herself as she set the bucket on a side table. It was clear to see that her mother-in-law was in her usual, sour mood, but Sassie had made up her mind to love everyone that morning and only think happy thoughts, so she forced a smile and inwardly prepared herself for the rest of the drill: *An' I hope you stripped Ruby's bag...*

Rosette said, "An' I hope you stripped Ruby's bag—else I'll haf to hear her bawl all day long."

Sassie knew the script by heart, could recite it word for word, as good as old Reverend Otis could recite the Ten Commandments. Every blessed day that the sun rose, the woman came at her with the same snippety remarks, just like clockwork. *An' did I thank to turn Ruby out?*

"Did you thank to turn her out?"

Why yes—yes, I did. "Yes, ma'am, I did all dem thangs you say, an' while I wuz at it, I went ahead on an' fed the chickens *an'* picked up the eggs." *Same as ever' other mawnin'.*

Rosette looked at her narrowly, trying to decide whether or not she was being smart with her, but she didn't say anything.

"Mama, can I have another biscuit?"

Sassie saw that Ellis had syrup on his chin but didn't bother wiping it off. "Can you say 'please'?" she chided mildly. She bent down and kissed him smackingly on the head before she dropped into her usual seat beside Obie.

"Pleeeeease...an' poke a hole in it," he said.

Sassie reached for a biscuit from the platter and poked a finger in it. Ellis's face broke into a big smile as she filled the hole with syrup. He took it from her and began devouring it greedily.

Rosette watched him silently for a minute; then she said, "You ax me, dey somethin' wrong wif dat boy." She scraped her chair back and went to the stove for more coffee. "He all time be eatin' like a hound—ain't big as nothin'. Needs a good wormin', you ax me."

Sassie looked back at her. *Now ax me what I thank you needs.* Trying to ignore her mother-in-law never seemed to work. She replied sharply, "*Wormin'!* Ain't nothin' wrong wif dis boy. Dis boy here healthy as a horse!"

Rosette came back to the table. "All I'z sayin', it'd be a waste of flour an' lard try an' fatten him up if his belly wuz full o' worms."

Sassie tossed her head. "Well, his belly *ain't.* He jus' don't set still long enough to get fat." She swore, if Ms. Quinn ever was to have something nice to say, she didn't know but what she wouldn't faint and fall out. She took another biscuit from the platter, and, with one swift slice of the butter knife, split it in two. *But seein' how ever' word come out yo' mouth cut like a blade...*

Rosette's mind suddenly shifted back to the jelly and Ezra. "I hear 'possums is bad to eat mayhaws. Yaw drag round too long, dey libel to beat us to 'em."

Knowing perfectly well he wouldn't hear the end of it until they went, Ezra swallowed the last of his biscuit and answered gravely, "Too much to do today. We'll go tomorrow." Whatever it took to cease his wife's nagging.

"Good," Rosette said, and almost smiled. "I'd just about walk to da state line an' back for a jar of jelly."

Sassie thought, *What a blessing it would be if she did an'...* But she told herself no and decided to leave it there.

The following afternoon, Ellis was lying on a pallet underneath the chinaberry tree in the backyard. Slyly, through half-closed eyes, he watched as his granny took the wash off the clothesline, putting the clothes in a wicker basket. He wanted to scratch his nose so bad, but knowing that she thought him to be asleep, he willed himself to lie perfectly still, waiting for her to go inside the house.

When the coast was clear, Ellis required only moments to steal across the yard and reach the path he'd seen his pawpaw and daddy go down a little while ago. Before venturing off to find them, he paused for a moment at the gap and glanced back at the house smugly, feeling clever for outsmarting his granny, since she wouldn't let him go. Not by an eye's flick had she noticed that he had been playing possum, and the notion that he had tricked her and snuck off without her knowledge pleased him. Quick as a rabbit, he turned and disappeared down the path.

Following the way the men had gone, Ellis walked steadily until he came to a place where the path forked, then, guessing which direction they might have taken, he veered off to the right. He made his way down the path quickly, expecting to happen up on them at any minute.

But he encountered no one. He had been dead wrong in the way he came.

Soon, Ellis found himself in the woods. When a squirrel somewhere up above on a tree limb scolded him, he stopped and looked around. Some instinct told him he was lost. He had no idea where he was or where his pawpaw and daddy were. The woods surrounding him made him feel suddenly small, and on edge. The squirrel chattered again, fussily.

Making his way as fast as he could, Ellis continued on the path a little farther. Finally, a familiar sight came into view. Realizing that he had been here before, he felt somewhat relieved. Still, he'd been told, rather *forbidden*, never, ever to come here alone. For a moment, he simply stood on the upper embankment of the river and stared down at it. Just below him was the spot where he and his pawpaw had come fishing that day. He saw the fallen log— half in, half out of the water—where he had dropped his line and caught that big catfish.

Ellis looked around. There was nobody there, no one to see him. The lure of the water drove all thoughts of danger from his young mind. And so, deaf to the strict orders of his parents and blind to whatever perils surrounded him, he ignored them all and went down the bank toward the water.

When he reached the water's edge, a school of minnows swimming in the shallows caught his attention immediately. He squatted down and leaned forward to get a closer look, watching them with fascination. Dragonflies darted and hovered over the water's surface, adding to the enchantment; a loggerhead turtle sunned on the drowned log. Completely engrossed in his surroundings, Ellis reached into the water for a pearly rock and then wiped his wet hand on the leg of his overalls.

Meanwhile, less than six feet away in the tall grass, yet another danger lurked. Detecting his scent, the snake had known the boy was there—long before the boy would become aware of the snake. While the minnows held Ellis's attention, the deadly cottonmouth held malevolently still, its tongue flickering in and out constantly, sensing the boy's every movement.

When it decided, the snake emerged from the reeds sleekly, noiselessly.

Precisely at that same moment, a blue jay flew overhead and screeched, seemingly to alert the boy. It seemed to say, "Snake! Snake! Snake!" Upon seeing the long, fat moccasin gliding across the ground toward him, Ellis's breath caught in terror. His body froze for a second as his mind filled with a sudden panic. Fear then sent him into a frenzied attempt to get away. Scrambling up from his squatting position, he turned and made a mad dash toward the embankment. Somehow, in all the hullabaloo, one of his shoes came off, causing him to lose his balance and fall. Frantically, he struggled to get up again. In his terrified mind, he could almost feel the snake's fangs sinking into his flesh. He made it to his feet, clumsily, then fell and tumbled backward— and rolled and rolled...and rolled.

Helpless to stop himself, Ellis rolled down the steep embankment and kept rolling until he rolled into the river.

"Yaw git down an' come set a spell," Rosette said when the wagon she had watched come all the way down the road circled around and came to a stop near the front porch.

"Afternoon, ma'am," Hiram said, hopping down from the seat, first lifting Nora out of the back, then helping Addie and Sassie down.

By now, it was almost two o'clock in the afternoon. When Hiram and Addie had chanced upon Sassie in town, Addie had insisted they give her a ride home from the Preacher's House, mainly to spend a little time visiting with her and too because she wanted to see Ellis and Star. Chatting and laughing, she and Sassie walked arm in arm toward the porch.

"Hello, Mrs. Quinn," Addie greeted her. "How are you feeling today?"

"Old an' wore out," Rosette replied.

Addie made herself smile.

Having just woken from her nap, Star had been drowsing on her grandmother's lap, but the instant she saw Nora, she climbed down, ready to play. "Come to me, pretty baby!" Addie swooped and grabbed the child, giving her a fierce hug. Star twisted and squirmed, freeing herself and scooting away, eager to explore the yard with Nora. Without anyone having clearly designated him to do so, Hiram took in behind the girls, acting as their watchful chaperon and leaving the three women to each another.

"I declare, it's like we don't even exist," Addie said. As she watched Star toddle along after Nora, she added, her voice a bit wistful, "Doesn't seem possible she's already old enough to be walking."

Rosette hollered at them from the porch, "Yaw stay out of my flower bed!"

Looking around, Addie asked, "Where's my Ellis?"

"He asleep on a pallet out back,' Rosette said. "Dem girls be done woke him in a minute, an he'll come runnin', scart he gone miss somethin'."

Sassie was frowning. "Ellis don't ever take a nap. He must be sick."

"He ain't sick. He mad," Rosette replied. "He showed out somethin' terr'ble 'cauze he didn't git to follow behin' dem mens gone to pick mayhaws. I'z scart he'd git on a snake back in dere, made him stay home wif me."

"Mmmm, mayhaw jelly," Addie interjected quickly, and satisfied with Rosette's explanation about Ellis, Sassie plopped down on the edge of the porch, letting her legs dangle.

For twenty minutes or so, the women sat on the porch and talked, mostly about canning recipes and the children. Addie had come to tolerate Rosette fairly well, so long as she took her in small doses. The woman did have a penchant for rubbing folks the wrong way—she surely would never be awarded a crown for hospitality—and the way she treated Sassie irked Addie to no end. Therefore, Addie considered it a godsend when Hiram rounded the corner of the house a short time later, swinging a little girl under each arm, both of them giggling with delight.

She stood and said, "Well, we must get home, but I really would like to see Ellis for a minute before we go." She loved both Sassie's children, but she had a special tenderness in her heart for Ellis. She looked at Hiram inquiringly. "Did you see him anywhere?"

He shook his head. "No."

"But y'all jus' got here," Sassie said. "Please stay longer." Jumping off the porch, she said, "I'll go find Ellis an' tell him you're here." They all followed her around the house, and as soon as she was in the backyard, she began calling, "Ellis! Ellis! Where are you?" They all looked about expectantly. When there was no response, she yelled louder, "Ellis Quinn! You better come to dis house when I call you!" But he was nowhere to be seen; the pallet under the chinaberry tree was unoccupied.

"He bound to be round here somewhere," she said

"He know to stay close," Rosette added.

"He *know*, but we all know what a little devil he can be. Mos' times it take a switch to make him do right."

"Perhaps he's hiding," Addie suggested.

"Why don't I go look for him in the barn," Hiram offered. "He probably ran off down there to get away from these girls." Addie nodded in agreement.

"I hate to put you to da trouble—"

"No trouble," Hiram said. "It won't take but a minute." He walked down the slope toward the barn, an old blue tick hound leading the way. He looked inside the tack room—*plow lines, mule collars, tools, barrels*—and in the dusty corncrib, and in every stall. Next, he climbed the ladder to the loft; it smelled like moldy hay and cottonseed. The sun was brilliant, and it shone through the cracks in the walls; over in one corner, a checkered hen sat trancelike on a nest of eggs in an old bushel basket. But there was no sign of the boy. Hiram climbed down the ladder, and all eyes were on him as he emerged from the barn and headed back across the yard. Shaking his head, he said, "He's not down there."

Addie looked at Sassie and asked, "Has he ever gone off before without telling anyone?"

Sassie nodded. "One time, when we first moved out here, he took off up the road pretty as you please to Auntie Beulah's without tellin' a livin' soul." She wiped her hands on the front of her dress and sighed. "I reckon I'll walk up to her house an' see if he's there." It was logical to think he might have gone there, since he'd done so before. As she started toward the road, she called back over her shoulder, saying, "When I git my hands on him, I fixin' to fo'evermo' blister his butt fo' sneakin' off an' worryin' us like dis!" She was trying not to appear overly alarmed, leastwise not yet.

Rosette turned to Addie and asked, "Miz Addie, would you an' Mr. Hiram drank some coffee?" There was a vague something in the way she said it, a touch of worry in her voice.

Addie smiled and politely accepted. Making coffee would provide a distraction for her, give her something useful to do while they waited for Sassie to return with Ellis.

When Rosette went inside the house to make the coffee and they were by themselves, Addie asked Hiram, "What are you thinking?"

He shrugged. "Knowin' Ellis, I figure he snuck off to follow Ezra an' Obie. It's likely he's with them. Soon as Sassie comes back, if he's not with her, I'll go try an' find them down in the woods, just to ease ever'body's mind."

Sassie returned fifteen minutes later, without Ellis. "Auntie Beulah said she ain't seen Ellis since las' Sunday." Her throat felt tight as she said his name. She was starting to feel afraid that something had happened to him, but she was fighting to control her emotions, knowing that she needed to just stay calm, keep looking, and find him.

Hearing the anxiety in Sassie's voice, Addie assured her with a gentle smile and said, "I'm sure Ellis is all right. I've no doubt we're going to find him. He'll probably come running around the house any minute now, screaming like a banshee." In light of her own apprehension, she instantly regretted her choice of words, given what a banshee was fabled to be.

Just then, they spied Ezra and Obie coming around the corner of the smokehouse carrying two buckets filled with mayhaws. Much to their dismay, they immediately noticed that Ellis wasn't with them.

Sassie hurried to meet them, with Hiram and Addie close behind.

As soon as Obie saw the look on her face, he asked, "What's the matter?" He knew whatever it was had to be serious. The expression on her face looked as bleak as a January morning.

"Have y'all seen Ellis?" Sassie asked.

Obie looked confused. "What? No. Ellis didn't go wif us." Looking around, he asked, "Why? Where is he?"

"We don't know," Sassie cried. "We wuz hopin' he was with y'all! I've called an' called, but he didn't come. I done been up to Auntie Beulah's..." Her voice trailed off.

Everyone seemed to be talking at once then. And nothing anyone was saying made any sense to Obie. No one seemed to know for sure how or what had happened, just that Ellis was missing. His mind was racing so, he knew he had to slow it down, or else he would never be able to figure it all out.

"How long he been gone?" he asked.

They each looked from one to another, speculatively. "We've been looking for him at least an hour."

An hour! How could such a thing happen!

Obie's reaction was immediate. "Ellis! Ellis!" Suddenly acting like he had gone crazy, he started out across the yard, calling Ellis's name. "Ellis! Where are you, Ellis? Come here to me, son!" He crisscrossed the length of the yard several times, calling out for him over and over. To settle it in his own mind, he did another quick search of the barn and sheds. *A tired little boy could fall asleep anywhere.* But Ellis wasn't there.

Returning to the others, he looked at them and laughed nervously, falsely, and echoed Sassie's earlier statement. "Well, he bound to be round here somewhere! He couldn't've jus' disappeared!" He had a sense that Ellis should just walk around the house any second now, acting like he was starving to death, wanting somebody to fix him something to eat.

"I'm tellin' you, we've looked everywhere," Sassie told him.

Word traveled quickly from one house to the next, and within minutes, two of Obie's cousins, Jasper and Zeke, were there, volunteering to help with the search. They slapped Obie on the back and shoulders, roughly, awkwardly, as men do when expressing concern and offering encouragement to other men.

Finally, knowing that it had to be said, Hiram spoke the words that no one wanted to hear: "We've looked everywhere on the premises, but we haven't looked in the woods yet."

Hearing this, Obie thought his heart would burst in his chest. It was a horrifying thought, thinking that his little boy might be all alone and lost, somewhere in the woods or, worse, in the swamps along the Leaf River. An awful sense of dread crept into his heart as he began in his mind cataloguing all the potential dangers—ravines, snakes, *the river*. He squeezed his eyes shut for a moment as though to clear the vision from his head, then opened them, and looked at Hiram. They all knew what had to be done, it only remained to do it.

In a quavering voice, he said, "We wastin' precious time standin' round here talkin'." They had a lot of ground to cover, and they had already lost an hour—that they knew of.

All this time, Ezra had said nothing. His face was like stone, his heart atremble.

Pulling Hiram aside and leaning in close enough so that no one else could hear but him, Addie asked, "Should I send after Wesley and Daniel? They could be of help. So might Jesse and Asher." As soon as she said it, she realized her mistake and corrected herself, given the manner in which Anna died. "I'm crazy, forget I said Asher."

There was a short pause before Hiram answered. "Let's wait," he said quietly. "Dependin' on what happens"—it was hard for him to say the words—"in case we end up havin' to search the river...at that point, we'd need some men that could swim." He didn't have to spell it out. She understood the drift of his thinking. He was silently praying that they would find a boy, not a body.

As the men readied to leave, Obie went to Sassie. As scared as she felt, she felt worse for him. Seeing the look in his eyes, the tears on his face, it all went straight to her heart. Her throat ached with love and pity for him, yet she made no move to comfort him.

She knew she must, and he must keep as composed as possible, for Ellis.

She gave him a trembling smile and held out her hands to him. Obie took them and kissed them; his tears fell upon them. With no spoken words, except through tears and touch, each felt what the other was feeling; they knew and understood the other's hope—and the other's dread. Letting go of Obie's hands, Sassie managed only to say, "Go on now, bring our boy home." It was the merest whisper, but Obie heard her loud and clear.

The men set out solemnly as though a leaden weight had settled on their hearts. As Obie walked along, all he could see was his young son's face, all he could hear was his voice. He started thinking about the day Ellis was born…the day he started walking… the first time he said *da-da*. He thought about everything they'd done together in three, now almost four years. Ellis was always so happy and so busy, so mischievous—so *alive*. If not for him, his life would be so empty. *If anything happened to him…*

As a new wave of fear washed over Obie, he knew he could not go on without him—without *Him*. Overwrought, he fell to the ground on his knees and cried out His name, begging Him to put a hedge of protection around Ellis, begging for strength and for courage… *Be of good cheer: it is I; be not afraid…* In that instant, Obie felt God's presence surround him. All at once He was in front of him, beside him, holding him, reassuring him… Deep inside, Obie knew that the Lord had been right there with him all the while, watching, waiting – *and he would have passed him by* – just waiting for him to call upon His name.

As he rose to his feet, very softly, very brokenly, Obie began singing "Jesus, Keep Me Near the Cross." One by one, the other men took up the hymn, until all of them were singing with him, or at least trying to. And as they sang, the words of the song as they drifted across the peaceful, green field were like a hopeful benediction: "Near the cross, I'll watch and wait, hoping, trusting ever…till my raptured soul shall find, rest beyond the river…"

Twisting her hands in her apron, Rosette watched the scene unfold from the kitchen window. Feeling ashamed, she reproached herself for not going out there as soon as she saw Ezra and Obie return, but at the same time, she was too ashamed to face them. She knew by now there was no doubt in any of their minds that Ellis's disappearance was all her fault. They knew it, as well as she knew it. It was she, and she alone, who was to blame for this whole, terrible ordeal, this nightmare. Naturally, they would want to know how she could have let such a thing happen, and how could she? After all, she was supposed to be watching him, and didn't. So what explanation could she give them? What could she possibly say that would make any difference now?

As she stood there at the window, her mind took her back to earlier in the day. She thought about Ellis and how bad he had wanted to go with Ezra and Obie. He had pitched an unholy fit when they left; bucking and carrying on so, she'd had to threaten him with a switch to get him to simmer down. After that, he fell asleep on the pallet. Sleeping, his face had looked so peaceful… so innocent.

She then thought about what happened later, when they were all in the backyard looking for Ellis, about when Mr. Graham had gone to look for him in the barn. While they were standing there, she could tell that Sassie was trying her best to stay calm, but she had seen that her hands were shaking. Then when Mr. Graham came out of the barn without Ellis, Sassie had looked straight at her, and though she had not said anything, she could tell that she blamed her for him being lost—and rightly so, because she was supposed to have been watching him. Sassie had entrusted her boy to her, and now her boy was missing. Now she would probably never trust her with him again, and she wouldn't blame her. After all, what kind of grandmother was she, to have let such a terrible thing happen?

And what kind of mother-in-law was she? She felt a pang of remorse.

Sometimes there were things people didn't like to admit about themselves, ugly things, and she knew that she hadn't always treated Sassie the way she should. Before Sassie and Obie had married, she had been mean to her, ugly. She had said some of the meanest, ugliest things about her, and to her. Truth be told, Sassie had turned out to be a good wife to Obie, and she was a good mother to Ellis and Star.

Funny, Rosette thought, the things that could pop into one's mind. She had suddenly remembered that blue pie plate that Sassie had given her a few years back, on Thanksgiving Day; it was one Georgianne had made. And what had she ever given Sassie, except grief?

Suddenly, the walls seemed to be closing in on her, she felt as though she was suffocating. She knew that Sassie and Obie would never be able to forgive her if something happened to Ellis.

And she would understand if they couldn't.

And Ezra—to him the sun rose and set in Ellis. How would he ever go on if something bad happened to him?

Tears rolled down Rosette's cheeks, tears of guilt and shame, pain, and regret. She had been negligent, and because of it Ellis, their precious little Ellis, was lost, perhaps even dead. And if he was dead, she would be the one responsible for killing him. And for that, she would never forgive herself. That would be a burden she would have to carry the rest of her life—that because of her own carelessness, her precious little grandson died.

In a haze of despair, Rosette staggered blindly from the kitchen and down the hall to her bedroom, where she fell to her knees at the foot of her bed. There was nothing she could do now but pray for her grandson's safety, and that he would be found, alive. *Please, God, let him be alive.*

A few minutes later, she heard a sound at the door. When she lifted her head, she saw Sassie was standing there, watching her. Her face was unreadable, almost without expression. She wondered if she was in shock. She could hardly bear to look at her, knowing the agony she must be feeling, and knowing that she was to blame for it. She wanted more than anything to tell her, to somehow be able to make her believe, how genuinely, genuinely sorry she was.

Finally, in big, gulping sobs, Rosette said the words that had been torturing her for hours: "I'z sorry...so very, very sorry. Dis all my fault...I should've been watchin' him...forgive me...oh, please, *please* fo'give me..."

Yes, it is your fault. It's your fault, in the first place, for harping on the mayhaws, and your fault for not letting Ellis go with his daddy and Mr. Ezra to start with. Your fault that he was outside, laying on a pallet... your fault for not watching him. It's your fault he's not here with us this very minute.

Sassie went and sat down on the floor beside her mother-in-law. "It ain't nobody's fault," she said. She put her arms around Rosette and pulled her close, letting her sob against her chest. Rosette clung to her while Sassie stroked her hair, and for a long time, the two of them held each other and rocked, consoling each other.

Entering Sassie's bedroom, Addie found her folding a pile of clothes that had been laundered that morning. "I was wondering where you got off to," she said. "Here, let me help you." She sat down on the bed, and the two of them worked silently for a few minutes.

"How are you holding up?" Addie asked softly. She was concerned. She knew Sassie had to be just hanging on by a thread, yet she appeared completely calm and collected.

Sassie sighed and said, "Fine, I reckon. I jus' be glad when they get back...po' Ellis mus' be starvin' by now." She could hardly bear thinking about where he might be, and what he must be feeling...*lost, scared, hungry.*

Addie smiled at her sympathetically.

When Sassie stepped toward the dresser with a stack of clothes, Addie couldn't help noticing the quilt on the bed. It was the star quilt that she, Claire, and Creenie had made several years back, when they all still lived in Collinsville.

Smoothing it gently with her hand, she said, "My, my, if this old quilt could talk...now there would be a story."

Her mind wandered back to those Saturdays when the three of them would meet up at Claire's house to work on the quilts. They had stitched two quilts that fall, with the initial intent of selling them to Mr. Neelson at the mercantile and dividing the money. But then, near the end of November, on Thanksgiving Eve, Addie's house had burned, forcing her to move here and live with Wesley and Laura, leaving the star quilt little more than half-done. Claire and Creenie had finished the quilts, and in the end, Claire had surprised her, giving them both to her at Christmas that year. Addie, in turn, passed the star quilt along to Sassie, after Creenie's death the following spring. *With all that happened, it's a wonder they ever got finished at all,* Addie thought.

While each of the three women had known they had been given a special gift in one another, they had not known, at least not at the time, that God had brought them together for a much bigger, more complex reason. All the while, as they sewed and ate pound cake, He was preparing them for events forthcoming that would touch and change each of their lives forever—indeed, events that would have infinite reverberations for generations to come.

Presently, as Addie sat reliving some of the joys and sorrows they had shared – seemingly so briefly – in her mind she could see their faces and...*a single, plump tear rolled down Creenie's cheek and left a wet line on the side of her face...*

All of a sudden, Addie tensed as she remembered something, something that Creenie had told her and Claire one day when they were quilting. The story was so tragic that upon hearing it, Addie could not think of what to say. She felt pensive now as the words reechoed in her mind: *I had a brother named Isaiah...he fell in da river, drown when he wuz three...* Creenie had gone on to tell them about how her daddy had jumped in the river to save Isaiah, and he too had drowned.

Addie shuddered at the remembrance.

She looked up at Sassie, said nothing, but when their eyes met, it was almost like Sassie could read her mind. Her eyes shining with unshed tears, Sassie shook her head in denial. She refused to allow herself—her *hope*—to be swept away on a current of ancient memories. All that had happened in another lifetime—someone else's lifetime, to someone else's baby.

"I know what you thankin'," she said, "but it ain't like that. Ain't no way my Ellis iz gone. If my baby wuz gone, don't you thank I'd know it—*feel* it—in *here?*" She poked a trembling finger at her chest. "I *know* my Ellis out dere somewhere in dem woods...an' he *alive.* We jus' gots to be patient an' wait on dem mens to brang him home." She simply could not bring herself to think otherwise. She knew Obie would bring Ellis back to her.

In a quavering voice, she added, "Anyhow, ain't God done promised us in da Bible He won't put nothin' on us we cain't handle? An' He *know* I couldn't handle losin' my baby."

The way Sassie looked at her, the way she said it, Addie wished with all her heart that she was right. While the Scripture does say that the Lord will not tempt one above that which he is able, Addie knew that God had a deeper, more intimate understanding of Sassie and of "that which she was able" than Sassie did. She also knew that no matter what lay ahead, God would see Sassie through it; He would see them all through it.

Not wanting to upset her further, Addie rose from the bed, and with as much enthusiasm as she could muster, she said, "Well, if Ellis is going be as hungry as you say, we'd best go out to the kitchen and start supper."

Beyond that, there was nothing else for them to do, except wait…and *pray*.

The five men—Obie, Ezra, Hiram, Zeke, and Jasper—walked for about fifteen minutes before coming to the juncture where the path split, where two trails branched out in opposite directions. Since Obie and Ezra had recently trod the one leading to the back field, by unspoken agreement, they took the one to the right, leading to the river.

Lined with tall grass and weeds, the trail was too narrow for them to walk side by side; Hiram led the way, the others following in succession; as they went along grasshoppers and small birds sprang up out of the brush. The men had only walked a little piece down the trail when they came to a low spot with a sandy bottom. Look there, Hiram pointed. They noted tracks in the sand, small shoeprints, leaving no doubt in their minds that Ellis had come that way.

Thus certain, the small party advanced, now spreading out but keeping in sight of one another. The open field soon gave way to the woods. Picking their way carefully through the thick underbrush, every twenty paces or so, they would stop, call Ellis's name, and cock their heads to listen for an answer. *Walk. Stop. Call. Listen.* It was a tense, painstaking process. As they drew near to the river, the smell of it drifted through the air toward them. *Walk. Stop. Call. Listen.* The warbling of birds fell silent each time they called.

Zeke was the first one to reach the ridge above the river. The water below him was a dingy brown, with clumps of yellow foam floating along down-current.

"Obie!"

The sound of Zeke's voice set off an alarm in the other men's minds. Filled with a terrible sense of foreboding, they ran to where Zeke was standing. With his hands at his sides, Zeke avoided Obie's eyes. He took a ragged breath like he was going to say something, but he couldn't say anything; he only turned his gaze toward the river. From the look on his face, no one wanted to look in that direction for fear of what they might see.

In the moment that followed, the air around them ceased to stir.

Obie went tearing down the embankment, stumbling every step of the way. Falling on his knees at the water's edge, he reached down and picked it up, his hand shaking uncontrollably. It was a shoe—a small, brown shoe. *Ellis's shoe.*

Suddenly, everything around him began to spin. He was dizzy, and it felt like the wind had suddenly been knocked out of him. Staggering to his feet, he began shouting, "Ellis! Ellis!" His legs were shaking and would hardly hold him up. He stared out across the breadth of the river, then downstream, his eyes desperately scanning the landscape for some sign of his boy. "Ellis! Ellis!" Like a madman, he hollered until he was hoarse. With agony on their faces, the other four men stood on the upper bank, feeling helpless and sick, wishing there was something they could do to make the situation better, or different, or all right, but they knew there was nothing, so they didn't even try.

After a few minutes, Hiram went to Obie. He touched his shoulder and squeezed it slightly to get his attention. "Maybe we should go back to the house, Obie, gather up a few more men to help us look. It'll be gettin' dark directly..." There was sorrow in his voice; he had little hope that Ellis, so small, could have survived the deep water and strong current of the river.

It was hard for Obie to focus on what Hiram was saying. What did he mean, go back to the house? He buried his face in his hands, trying to clear his thinking. Go back, why? Finally, he looked over at Hiram and asked incredulously, "Man, iz you gone crazy?" He looked from one of the men to the other. Then holding the shoe up for all of them to see, he said, "Yaw thank I'z fixin' to jus' leave up out o' here an' go back to da house wif nothin' 'sept dis shoe in my hands?" He shook his head. "Naw, man. What I gone tell Sassie, after she done tol' me, 'Obie, go brang our boy home'?" All he could think was that he would be leaving his son behind, all alone.

Obie's mouth was dry, his lips, trembling. He didn't even realize he was crying as he stood there with tears coursing down his cheeks, staring at the other men, begging them with his eyes to somehow help him. He had no idea what to do next. He was in desperate need of some encouragement, some hope.

Trying to fight back their own despair, the others could only watch silently, their eyes blurred by tears as Obie started up the bank, again calling out for Ellis. Ezra's face was filled with such anguish and was so pale that he looked as if he might fade away at any moment. As Obie hollered for Ellis, the old man bowed his head and began mumbling a prayer. "Please, God, help us…O, help us, God…help us." He kept saying it over and over.

"Ellis! Ellis!" the cries continued, rising hoarsely from Obie's throat.

And then, at long last, from somewhere in the woods, there came a faint, almost indistinct cry. Almost sure that they had heard something, each man glanced around at the others for affirmation that they had heard it too. They stared into the trees, straining their ears. Everything seemed to stop for an endless moment.

Then, they heard it again.

"Daddy!"

"Ellis!" Obie yelled, now running toward the sweet sound. The others followed, calling out, laughing and crying all at the same time, "Ellis! Ellis!"

"Daddy!"

When Ellis came into view, Obie was there. Letting out a strangled cry, he lifted his son into his arms and hugged him, kissing his face, his hair, his eyes. "Thank you, God, thank you, God, thank you, God," he cried over and over. It was a miracle! His son was alive! Ellis had been found!

"Dere wuz a big snake, Daddy," Ellis was saying weakly, "an' I fell in da river...den I got up an' I ran, an' I ran, an' I ran. Den I hid so the snake couldn't find me." He patted Obie's cheeks. "Iz you cryin', Daddy? Why iz you cryin'?"

Obie hugged him tighter and laughed. "'Cause I'm so happy to see you. We thought you wuz lost...I thought I had lost you." He couldn't hold his son close enough.

Then all at once everyone was circled around, touching, patting, wanting assurance that he had indeed been found and was all right. Ellis had nary a skinned place on him; besides for his clothes being wet and dirty, and for the fact that he was wearing only one shoe, he seemed unscathed by the whole ordeal. Confused by all the attention, he put his head on Obie's shoulder and whimpered tiredly, "Daddy, I'z hungry."

He had had a great adventure, but now it was over, and he was ready to go home.

Soon after, the chicken had been taken up, the rice was done, Addie had slid a pan of biscuits into the oven, and Sassie was browning flour in the chicken drippings to make gravy. The smell of their cooking was enticing.

Addie took off her apron and poured herself a glass of sweet tea. She went outside on the back porch where she was sure nobody would be, and stood looking. A few feet away, Nora and Star were sitting on the ground beneath an aged cedar tree, digging in the dirt with rusty spoons. With the sun descending into the west and day fleeing, the cedar's shadow had begun to lengthen, slanting down the grassy slope toward the barn. Addie could see the chickens in the barnyard, scratching and pecking, a brood of biddies racing about on spriglike legs. A Negro boy was perched atop the rail gate that led from the yard to the fields, using it as a lookout for the men.

Voices drifted around from the front of the house where, during the course of the afternoon, a small crowd had gathered and stayed, waiting on news of Ellis. Cane-bottomed chairs and rockers were strung from one end of the porch and yard to the other, and in her mind, Addie could imagine them rocking to and fro, to and fro...*like spectators awaiting a grand performance.* Some of the young girls were jumping rope, chanting a ditty: "Three-six-nine, da goose drank wine, da monkey chewed tobacco on da street car line, da line broke, da monkey got choked, an' dey all went to heaven in a little rowboat..."

Good for them, Addie thought. Much had happened in the last few hours, her nerves had been near the skin all afternoon, and she was dead tired, both physically and mentally. Wanting to feel as much space and silence around her as possible, needing the solitude, she was grateful just to have this moment to herself. Resting her head against a post, she closed her eyes and listened. A long way off, a pair of mourning doves called and answered, their cries so soft and throaty, fading and rising—*fading and rising.*

"Dey comin'! Dey comin'!"

Addie's eyes flew open. For an instant, she felt her whole body go stiff. Seeing the boy jump off the fence and start running, she looked out across the field. At first, she didn't see anything. And then suddenly, she saw a figure come into view, *Zeke,* then another, *Jasper.* She stood on the top step, holding her breath. And then—she would never forget what she saw then—she saw them—Ezra, Hiram, and Obie—emerge from the shadowy end of the field. Her heart soared. Laughing through her tears, she shouted, "Sassie! Sassie!" as she began to run across the yard. There were shouts and cheers of jubilation, and for a moment, she couldn't see him for her tears, but Ellis was there, waving at them, shining out like a beacon, looking proud and important astride his daddy's shoulders.

It was the finest sight anyone could imagine.

There was rejoicing, oh, there was!

Late into the night, long after everyone had fallen asleep, Ezra slipped out of bed and made his way slowly down the hall to Ellis's room; it was a full moon, and there was enough light for him to see by.

Ellis lay on his back, sound asleep, with the sheet twisted around his legs. As Ezra stood watching his grandson's sleeping face, and listening to him breathe, he felt a love so strong, so primordial that he couldn't help but wonder if other pawpaws cherished their grandchildren as much as he cherished his, but surely, that wasn't possible. He loved Ellis and Star with every ounce of his soul and would give his life for them. Ever so carefully, he reached down and straightened the cover. Placing his hand on Ellis's chest, he felt his heart beating, young and strong. Just hours earlier, he had feared the boy gone. *If anything had happened to him...* But blinking his eyes dry, Ezra forced the thought from his mind and mouthed silently, gratefully, *Thank you, Father God, fo' sparin' dis boy's life...*

Suddenly realizing the selfishness of his prayer, he bowed his head and whispered, "Thank you, Father God, fo' lovin' me so much dat you gave yo' only begotten Son to die fo' my sin." What an awesome sacrifice, what an awesome gift, what a great and awesome love...

Finishing his prayer, Ezra went over to the chair near the window and sat down heavily. It had been a long and brutal day, and he was exhausted. Yawning, he looked out the window. The moon was bright, the place was still, the house, quiet. He leaned his head back and closed his eyes. As his mind drifted toward slumber, he called up that day when he and Ellis had last sat on the bank of the river and fished, the day Ellis caught that big catfish. From this thought he took joy and smiled.

A minute later, smiling still, Ezra dropped off to sleep, the sound of his snores mingling together with the sound of Ellis's soft, even breathing.

At daybreak when Obie entered the room, Ezra's head was tilted back in peaceful repose, his hands lay folded on his lap. At first glance, he looked as though he were peacefully sleeping. But as Obie approached him, he saw and knew, and the truth of it almost choked him, for during the night Ezra had crossed over Jordan, and Obie, as he wept, reached out and clung to his father's body in vain, seeking life that was no longer there.

CHAPTER 23

Whither shall I go from thy spirit, or whither shall I flee from thy presence?

—*Psalms 139:7 (*KJV*)*

*I*t seemed like everybody in the community turned out for church that Sunday morning. A warm and welcoming place, Harmony Baptist Church was not really all that large, with no more than forty members on the roll. The church house itself sat in a little hollow surrounded by sycamores and sweetgums and was made of clapboard that had been painted white. Inside the church, it smelled of varnish and beeswax; the floor was planked-oak; there were eight pews on either side of the aisle and a woodstove in one corner for heat during the winter months.

The preacher's name was Rev. J. D. Higgins, and Maude Thorne had been the church organist for as long as anyone could remember. Maude was a bit of a fuss-pot, but extremely talented. She played in such a way that gave breath to every note, giving the music such life that it almost became visible to the eye.

When the singing was over, Brother Higgins took the pulpit, and after he prayed, he told the congregation to turn in their Bibles to the book of Jonah. He began reading with the first chapter:

> Now the word of the Lord came unto Jonah, the son of Amittai, saying, "Arise!"

For emphasis, he pounded the pulpit and shouted, "Get up!"

The words clapped like thunder in Daniel's head.
The preacher continued reading the passage:

> "But Jonah rose up to flee unto Tarshish from the presence of the Lord, and went down to Joppa; and he found a ship…and he went down into it."

Brother Higgins pointed out how the Scripture said repeatedly that Jonah went *down,* and how that is the direction one goes anytime they attempt to run from God. In comment to Jonah's futile hope of distancing himself from the Lord's presence, he went on to reference the writings of David in the book of Psalms: "If I ascend up into Heaven, thou art there: if I make my bed in hell, behold, thou art there…"

It was a powerful sermon, one meant especially for Daniel, but Daniel wasn't listening. Rather, like Jonah, he found himself trying to flee the insistent voice inside his own head and heart. God's voice was calling his name, commanding him to obey His call, demanding an answer, *tossing him about…*

Daniel was miserable. He stirred in the pew uneasily, then leaned forward with his hands clasped together, his elbows on his knees. He looked *down* at the floor. His head felt hot, like it might burst into flames at any moment. He could feel Amelia's eyes pressing *down* on him wonderingly, but he didn't look at her.

"What about you?" Brother Higgins was saying. "Will you obey God's call and dedicate your life, your all, to Him?" An interminable hush seemed to fall in the church, the question seemingly wanting for an answer. To Daniel, it seemed like the question had been asked directly to him and that everybody had turned and was looking at him, waiting for him to answer. He hoped he wouldn't be sick and make a fool of himself in front of the whole church. Finally, thank God, the song leader went up and called out a hymn number, and as Maude began to play, everyone stood. The preacher said, "If God is speaking to your heart today, I urge you to come forward as we sing the invitational."

Daniel stood on trembling knees. *"Almost persuaded..."* As the song filled the church, he could feel the Spirit drawing him, prompting him to go forward. *"Almost persuaded..."* There was no doubt in his mind what he needed to do. God was calling, and he needed to step out, walk down the aisle, and take the preacher's hand, or at least go kneel at the altar. *"Almost persuaded..."* He could feel the nearness of the Lord, watching, waiting as he gripped the back of the pew in front of him. He was squeezing *down* on it so tightly that he expected to look *down* and see the imprint of his hands embedded in the wood. *Lord, You know I can't... You know I'm not worthy.* Though his soul was in turmoil, Daniel held back. After all, wasn't the choice his? Hadn't God given him free will to choose? He didn't have to do anything he didn't want to do. *"Go, Spirit, go Thy way..."*

At long last, the song came to an end, and Brother Higgins called on one of the deacons to lead them in a closing prayer.

Not surprisingly, the wood beneath Daniel's fingers felt cold.

Daniel had taken the dog Jonah with him a time or two into Oakdale and inquired around town as to whether any had made mention of losing a dog that fit his description. None had. Nor did anyone know of any person thereabout named Jonah.

Jonah soon became Daniel's constant companion, waiting at the door for him to emerge in the mornings, and sleeping on the porch, guarding the front door at night. It became a natural sight for him to go with Daniel to the woodshop, and he would even ride to church in the wagon with them on Sundays and sit outside the church-house during the services.

The dog tolerated the affections of Amelia and the children well enough, but he was no one's but Daniel's. After a while, Daniel never questioned the mystery of where the dog Jonah had come from, for in his heart, he knew.

CHAPTER 24

Be anxious for nothing, but in everything by prayer and supplication, with thanksgiving, let your requests be made known to God.

—Philippians 4:6 (KJV)

Following Ezra's unexpected death, for those who loved him life was different, but life went on. Having spent most of his days working alongside his father, Obie had become a knowledgeable and capable farmer, and with Ezra's passing, he assumed full charge of the farm. Giving thought to the future, he hired his cousins Jasper and Zeke to help him and started making plans to clear and utilize the back field. Once the second harvest was over, they would saw down the larger trees and drag them out by mules to cut and split to use as firewood; in the winter, they would put up new fence, and in the spring add a few more head of cattle. Sometimes Obie could not sleep at night for thinking of ways to make the farm more prosperous. *Something he would be proud to leave behind for his children when his time came.*

Another unexpected death that occurred around that same time was Ezra's sister-in-law, Beulah. Though she was eighty-one, she did not die naturally of old age but rather choked to death at the dinner table. She was eating a chicken wing and choked on a bone. It was unclear if the bone was the cause of her death, or if it was the wad of cornbread her daughter stuffed down her throat in an attempt to dislodge it that led to her demise.

It was now near the end of May. Whereas so much had happened during the past weeks—the ordeal with Wilkes, Ellis having been lost, and Ezra's dying—Addie was glad to finally have an opportunity to again sit down and read from Claire's journal. That night as soon as Hiram went to bed, she took it from the chest and went and sat where she could catch the light from the lamp. She opened it to the marked page and noticed, much to her disappointment, that she had only a few pages left:

June 19, 1865

My darling Luke has been home for a couple of weeks now. He just walked up in the yard one evening right at dusk-dark. At first I thought I was dreaming. I'd never seen a more pleasing sight, or a more sorrowful one. He looked so poor, like a walking skeleton, near starved to death, his face so drawn and thin. He'd been making his way home for near a month. His clothes were rags, his shoes cracked, his feet solid blisters. However tattered, he is alive, and there are no words to express my joy in having him back home. I thank the Lord for that, and that this long, wretched war is over.

General Lee surrendered on April 9. Lincoln was shot on the fourteenth. Luke said he was officially paroled from the army on the fourth of May. It's hard to believe after four long, hard, bloody years the war is finally over. All said and done, they say that more than half a million have perished, that one-fourth of all the men in the South and half of all livestock are dead. They speculate it will take at least twenty-five years just to replace the horses.

When Lincoln's Emancipation Proclamation became law, hundreds of freed slaves, with nowhere to go, ended up in a camp at Natchez Under-the-Hill. With unsanitary conditions and little food available to them, it is said they die at a rate of thirty a day, many of them women and children, and that they are buried in pits, on top of each other.

Again, I thank the Lord that this long, wretched war is finally over! It has left a deep and lasting mark on us all.

There is another soldier here with us too. When Luke introduced us, he told me plain and simple that he and this man had been to a place they "hoped not to revisit," which told me they seen a fair share alongside each other. He said he considers the man a friend above all friends, and me knowing Luke, that's a-plenty for me. I don't know how long he's thinking on staying, but he's welcome.

I've been pouring the feed to them, and they've been eating hard and sleeping hard ever since they got home. When the man walked up with Luke, he had a fiddle with him, and the way he plays could only be an anointing from God.

July 10, 1865

Luke came to me today with a story so utterly befuddling that I have to write it down in order to get it straight in my head. It's about the man that came back from the war with him, the one who's been staying with us for some weeks now. Seeing how things are headed, now that the man has decided to stay on and make Collinsville his home, Luke said I needed to know the truth about him. So, he and the man commenced to tell me.

As for the battle itself, they said only that it was the worst they had seen and that many a man fell that day. The man said more than half of his regiment was killed, and the rest of them were forced to retreat. He said amid all the gunfire and chaos, they scattered in every direction and that he got all turned around and separated from the rest of his men. He was lost, and he had lost his rifle and bayonet and had no weapon except for his bowie knife. He said he didn't know how long or how far he wandered through the woods looking for someone from his unit, but he never did find them or the peach orchard where they'd camped the night before. He said finally he was so tired and hungry he got to feeling defeated, in body and mind, and in spirit. He said he thought about just lying down, wondered how long it would take for him to die like that, without food or water, said he was dying a slow death anyway, so it didn't matter. Or how long might it be before the enemy came through and ended his life for him? He said then all of a sudden-like, he walked right up on another soldier, just sitting in the leaves, leaning against a big hickory stump. Oddest of things, he said, there was a fiddle lying across the man's lap, like he'd just finished playing it. His rifle was lying right beside him in the leaves, just an arm's reach away. He said the man didn't move, though, said he just stared at him. It took him a minute to realize that the soldier was actually dead, apparently had died with his eyes open. When he went over to him, he could tell he hadn't been dead all that long though. His canteen was still hanging around his neck. He figured it was likely the man had been wounded in the same battle he'd been fighting in earlier and made it that far before sitting down to die, maybe chose that particular spot, knowing it was to be his final resting place. He said he couldn't help but think that perhaps one of his own bullets had done this. The man said he just stood there for a while looking off into the woods, thinking within himself, his mind all in a fog about what to do next. Concluding he had nothing more to lose, he had about done decided to just give himself up to the other side and become a prisoner of war, citing that he'd become a captive of sorts anyway the day he signed up. But, he said, all of a sudden, out of the clear blue, an idea came to him. He said the next thing he knew, he was stripping off the dead soldier's uniform and, a minute later, shucking his own. He said he put on the man's gray trousers and butternut shell jacket, and his kepi, then hid his own Union blues up under a fallen log. He said when he reached down to take the man's rifle, without even thinking, he picked up the fiddle too. He said he covered the soldier up with a gum blanket and set out walking. When he came to a creek, he followed it, just hoping to find someone, anyone. After a while, he come up on Luke. Luke was by himself down by the creek, scouring out his plate in the sand. Luke said the minute he laid eyes on the man, despite the uniform, he knew he wasn't Confederate. And the man could tell he knew. But Luke said it didn't matter. He said when he looked into the man's eyes, he saw something, sensed a feeling of some kind, like there was some kind of kinship between them that he couldn't explain further. Luke had waxed lonesome to the war and its atrocities. It had poisoned him enough, he had lost enough of himself to it already, he said. But he had never, and would never let bureaucracy govern his idea of what made one man worth more than another. We are all, each of us, he said, souls traversing, passing through this earth for but a short while. It's where we go when we leave here that proves, or disproves, our ranks. There was no way, he said, that he would report this man.

With so much else to worry about, Luke figured it doubtful anyone would pay particular attention to yet another weary straggler. With all the chaos of war all around them, it was not of much importance. Every man's main concern was just trying to stay alive. But just the same, they worked up a story, just in case—that the man had got separated from his outfit and was mute from an old battle injury, one from when he fought in the Battle of Vicksburg. That night, he bedded down in Luke's camp like he was one of them. And come morning, he was.

Now, how do you like them apples?

Addie's pulse was racing. What an incredible story! She couldn't believe what she was reading or that Claire never thought to tell her this when she was living. Could this have really happened? But she knew it did, for who could make up such a tale? She continued reading:

August 5, 1865

Today, me and Luke, Samuel and Rachel sat down together to discuss for one last time the story we've all took a part in concocting. It is pure-and-T big enough to clog a cannon, but I guess at this point the truth would avail nothing. Not that he really talks all that funny, not so much of a twang that anybody would automatically peg him for a Yankee. I said, given enough time he'll sound ignorant as the rest of us, but I reckon what Luke said makes more sense, that it's better if we're all on the same page of this fairy tale. So, if anybody ever was to ask, we're just gonna say that he was from a place they hadn't been to before, like north Alabama. We don't know anybody in Collinsville that's ever been to that part of the country, so they wouldn't know the difference. It's unlikely anybody will ever ask, but if anyone does, it's also unlikely any of us will stutter over this lie. Only the four of us know different, and the four of us have made a pact never to tell.

Dalton Davis weren't never no count, not really. Never was a good husband, or a good father. I see things in Samuel, same as Luke. Samuel Warren is a fine man, regardless of where he came from. It all seems fitting— more like a godsend—that he and Rachel have fallen in love and are getting married tomorrow. I've nary a doubt he'll make a fine husband for Rachel and be a fine daddy to Wesley and little Addie.

Addie stared blankly at the page. For some reason that last passage had not registered clearly in her mind, something about it just didn't ring true. Thinking that she had misread it, she read it again for a second time, this time more slowly, paying particular attention to every word.

Dalton Davis weren't never no count, not really. Never was a good husband, or a good father. I see things in Samuel, same as Luke. Samuel Warren is a fine man, regardless of where he came from. It all seems fitting—more like a godsend—that he and Rachel have fallen in love and are getting married tomorrow. I've nary a doubt he'll make a fine husband for Rachel and be a fine daddy to Wesley and little Addie.

Addie felt her heart begin to pound. *What could this mean?* She still didn't understand. None of it made sense. Desperate to know more, she flipped the page. There had to be more, more of an explanation. But that was the last page, the end of the journal. Telling herself to remain calm, she went back to the preceding entry and started rereading once again. Her lips moved silently, her eyes moved across the page rapidly, nervously, like bees swarming around a threatened hive.

When she came to the end, she just sat there, staring at the words, completely addled. *I have truly gone mad,* she thought, *truly.* She needed someone to explain all this to her, but the only ones who could explain it were gone. *…only the four of us know….* Addie shook her head. It simply wasn't true. It was absurd. It had to be a lie. *Otherwise…* No! She couldn't believe it, *wouldn't* believe it. She thought, *Because if this was true…*

All of a sudden, she felt like a lost child. It was as though her whole world came crashing down, like everything she had ever believed had been a lie, her whole life had been a lie. *They* all had lied. *…and the four of us made a pact…* Her father, whom she loved with all her soul, Claire, who was supposed to have been her best friend, Luke, even her own mama—they, every one, were liars. An arrow of betrayal ripped right through her heart.

Addie felt as though she were going to pass out if she didn't get some air. With the journal still in her hands, she got up and went outside onto the porch. She just stood there, shaking, confused. She couldn't understand how they could do what they had done, how they could be so deceitful. They had made a complete falsity of her whole life, her family, not to mention her friendship with Claire. . . . *he'll be a fine daddy to Wesley and little Addie.* Mindlessly, without a word to anyone, she set out walking toward Wesley's house. She had no shoes, not even a wrapper over her nightgown.

When she reached the house, she went up the steps and knocked loudly on the door. Woken from a deep sleep, it took Wesley a few minutes to open it. The instant he saw her standing there in her nightclothes and bare feet, he asked, "Dear Lord, what's happened?" Obviously something, or why else would she be there in the middle of the night? in her nightgown? without any shoes?

Holding the journal out in front of her, she cried hysterically, "*This* is what's happened! They lied! Our father wasn't even our father! Our real father was hanged! The man we thought was our father was really a Yankee soldier! Come to find out, we aren't even Warrens!"

Still half-asleep, Wesley stared at her groggily. He wished he knew what the devil she was talking about, but not a word she was saying made a lick of sense. She looked and sounded a little crazed to him. "Where's Hiram?" he asked.

"*Who*? *Hiram*? He's home in the bed, asleep! Did you not hear a word I just said? Doesn't it bother you in the least to know our entire life has been a lie?"

"Addie, what are you talkin' about?" He yawned, not out of rudeness, but sleepiness.

"I'm trying to tell you!" she said impatiently, with tears in her eyes. "I need you to listen to me! It's all right here in Claire's journal! According to this, our father, our *real* father, was a man named Dalton Davis!" Her voice broke in a sob.

Addie was visibly shaken and pale, obviously very upset, and Wesley's sleepiness had suddenly been replaced with curiosity. "Come inside," he said, "but lower your voice. Laura an' the young'uns are tryin' to sleep." *Like most sane people.* She followed him into the kitchen. He lit a lamp, and they sat down at the table. "All right," he said, "start over, from the beginning."

For the next half hour, Addie flipped through the journal, letting Wesley read certain passages. When he reached the end and looked up from his reading, he took his time before commenting. It was all so incredible, near impossible for him to absorb.

Addie was studying his face. "Well, say something," she said.

Wesley ran his fingers through his hair, trying to sober himself. Finally, he said slowly, "I don't really know what to say, Addie. It's a lot to digest in one settin'." Another minute or two passed before he added realistically, "On the other hand, it's not the end of the world, an' I don't really see how any of this makes much difference now."

"What! How can you say that!" she cried incredulously. "Don't you even care that they lied to us! Our own mother and father!" How he could seem so unaffected by this discovery that had her reeling was beyond her. But that was a man for you, always able to just accept what was, spit, scratch, and go on.

Wesley answered honestly, "Well, if this is all true, an' I'm not sayin' it ain't, but if it is, it would seem fairer to say they hid the truth, rather than to say they lied, an' it sounds to me like they did it all for good reason. Otherwise, 'less I'm mistaken, all of us would have to own up to a fair share of lyin' ourselves."

In answer to the perplexed look she was giving him, he said, "Think about it, Addie. Remember the day Travis shot Alfred? Didn't we all decide—me, you, Laura, an' Hiram—that it was best not to tell the young'uns it was him, since they believed he was already dead? And didn't we also decide it was best they didn't know about him killin' Mama?"

"But…" That was not what she wanted to hear. She said, "But Claire and I were best friends. I always thought…" Her voice broke. Her heart felt so wounded and bruised.

Wesley replied, "Ask me, honorin' that pact just goes to show what kind of friend Claire really was. The way I see it, anybody has a friend like that, one that wouldn't betray a trust, ort-a count theirself lucky."

Everything Wesley said was true, especially about Claire, and thinking about her now made Addie all the more grateful to have had her for a friend. Claire had been so good to her, had always been there for her. Through her tears, Addie asked, "Still, aren't you even the least bit curious about our real father, or the least bit sad about Pa?"

In an attempt to make her smile, Wesley grinned and replied, "Sounds like that feller Davis weren't nothin' but a bona fide hellion—maybe that's where I get it from." Then he decided to be serious. "I reckon I'm bound to ponder all these things from time to time, I can't say I won't. However I can say, without any doubts, that there weren't no finer man than our pa. He was a good, kind, God-fearing man. He loved us and cared for us, and he was the best father anyone could ever have, so there ain't nothin' to be sad about there. According to Claire's journal, he *chose* to be our father. He chose to love us, chose to raise us, and as far as I'm concerned, *he* is my *real* father." It was an emotional moment for Wesley, because he not only loved Samuel, but now, after reading the account of his enduring will and survival during the war, he also had a new and deeper respect for both him and Luke.

Hearing him say all those things made tears flow down Addie's cheeks. She nodded and said, "I feel the same way." And she did. After all, she knew better than anyone it was love—not blood—that ordained a family. Without any regard to blood, Hiram was Daniel and Emily's father, and in their eyes, and in their hearts, they were his. Wiping her eyes, she said, "I loved Pa so."

"Well, do you love him any less now?" Wesley asked gently.

She looked over at him, shocked. "Of course not! What a ridiculous question! Pa meant the world to me, and I'll love him always, no matter what. Nothing could ever change that." It was an emphatic torrent of words, until her brother's eyes told her he'd made his point. "Oh," she said.

Wesley suddenly thought of something else. "I reckon this explains why Rebekah was the apple of Mama's eye." And why Rachel lost her mind when Rebekah died.

"Oh my goodness," Addie said. "I didn't think of that. But I do think of Rebekah sometimes, especially when I look at Meggie, the two of them looked so much alike as babies."

They sat and talked for another half hour. When Addie rose from her chair and started for the door, Wesley looked at her with tired worry and said, "I'll walk you home." But she smiled and shook her head. "Go to bed. I'll be all right." As she went down the steps, he called after her softly, "I'll see you tomorrow." She walked out across the yard, and the night enveloped her, and while he stood gazing off yonder into the starry, indigo sky, he heard her say, "Tomorrow."

It had not taken Hiram long to read the journal, and while he, like Wesley, found the story of how Samuel Warren came into being completely intriguing, looking at it through Addie's eyes, he could also understand why she was so upset. The timing was especially unfortunate, that she should learn of these things now, after Claire and anyone else who could have answered her questions were gone. As they talked, a tear crept down her cheek.

Hiram reached out and took her hand. "You all right?" he asked gently. Of course he knew she would be. They both knew she had been through much worse things than this, things that had, over time, only made her strong. Sometimes he was amazed at how, through it all, she had remained so steadfast, so unwavering in her faith.

"Not yet," she answered honestly, "but I will be." She looked sad as she said, "Isn't it crazy how one little sentence can turn a person's whole life bottom side up and inside out?" She didn't say it out loud but thought, *And rend the fabric of your heart right down the middle.*

Hiram thought about saying how crazy it would be if a person were to let one little sentence destroy a whole lifetime of good memories, but he didn't want to say too much. Addie was going to have to come to the realities of this situation herself. And he knew she would, given time. He just nodded quietly.

"I just keep wondering why Claire kept the journal," Addie said. "She had to have brought it with her when she moved here from Collinsville. She had to have known when she put it on that shelf it might someday be found."

Hiram said, "Maybe she wanted you to find it. Maybe she had always wanted to tell you the truth, but couldn't in good conscience because of the agreement she made with the others. Leaving it to chance might have seemed like a way for you to find out without her feeling like she'd betrayed them. Once she died, it wouldn't matter anymore."

Addie groaned. There were a thousand unanswered questions swirling around in her mind, and all they could come up with was hypothetical assumptions. She didn't want maybes and might-haves, she wanted facts. She cried, "Only now *their* past has come back to haunt *me.*"

Hiram could almost feel her frustration. He was sorry for her distress, but there was nothing he or she could do about any of it now. The answers she sought died with the four conspirators. He said wisely, "Even if their plan seems flawed to us, it's clear their intentions weren't. They never meant to hurt anyone." He paused a moment, looking into her tear-filled eyes. "You're gonna have to let this go, sweet." He stood then and put an arm around her shoulders, she nodding as he whispered into her neck that he loved her.

Before he went out, he said, "One thing I can say for sure— life is odd, or at least ours has been so far." He grinned at her, his eyes crinkling. "An' never dull. Ain't no tellin' what's libel to happen around here from one day to the next!" He was teasing her, and it worked. For the first time that morning, she smiled.

But Addie felt dejected. It had been a terrible shock to her, finding out that Samuel Warren wasn't her real father. She knew what Claire had written had to be true; however, she still could not accept it. During the daytime, when she was occupied in a myriad of ways and stayed busy, she was able to pretend what she had discovered didn't bother her as much as it did. But at night, in the dark hours when the house was sleeping, she would lay in bed wide-awake, besieged by questions and conflicting emotions, a maelstrom of memories whirling through her mind. She would spend hours thinking about the man who had been her father, and wondering about the father she had never even known existed, trying to sort it all out and piece it all together.

As she relived times past in her mind, among the things she thought about was her pa's kind nature, his caring ways, and his generosity. Samuel Warren had been a man who truly lived his life in the shadow of God's wings. He had loved the Lord, and he loved people; he was forever stopping by a neighbor's house; she, always tagging along. Some of her happiest hours as a girl had been spent with him. She remembered his hands—big, strong hands that could set most anything right, hands she'd held on to so tightly the night he died. She thought about how his love had consoled and reassured her when Rebekah died, and how he carried them all through the awful time that followed… and how he played his fiddle. It was like Claire had written: "The way he plays could only be an anointing from God." *The fiddle that had once lay across the lap of an unknown soldier…*

Addie had loved and admired Samuel with her whole heart, and as she lay awake night after night remembering the precious times they had shared, tears would slide from her eyes, and there would be a lonesomeness, an aching emptiness inside that almost overwhelmed her. She still missed him, and it almost hurt more now than the first time she lost him.

In the wee hours of the morning, before she would finally fall asleep, Addie's last thoughts were usually centered around Dalton Davis. She accepted that the man, whoever he was, had been her real father. Her flesh, at least, was his. It seemed only natural that she should be curious and want to know more about him. She would press her mind and try to remember anything that she might ever have heard anyone say, or even hint, about him, insofar as ever even speaking his name. But of course there was nothing, nothing of him at all. Even the chronicle in her mama's old Bible provided no clue, except for an unsightly ink stain that most likely blotted out the information she was searching for. She would find herself wondering if there might be anyone still living in Collinsville that might have known him, or known anything about his family.

After three nights of this, the stress of it all had worn Addie down. Getting up in the morning had become an effort. She was exhausted; her mind was as tired as her body. Saturday afternoon, she went into the parlor and stood before the fireplace. Above the mantel hung the old photograph taken many years ago of her, her mother and father, Wesley, and Rebekah. In it, Samuel stood handsome and noble-looking, as she realized he always would— in both her eyes and her heart. Maybe that was all that was really important, she thought. Maybe none of the rest really mattered after all. Forget about scribblings in family Bibles and carvings on headstones. The longer she thought about things, the clearer they became. She had been carrying around a senseless burden, and it was time she laid it aside. *All that worrying…*

The clock showed nearer to two o'clock than one. Addie went into the hallway and stood listening for a moment at Nora's door. Emily had come home during the semester break and Addie went to her room to tell her she was going for a walk. "Nora's down for her nap. Listen for her while I'm gone." There was somewhere she needed to go, someone she needed to talk to.

As she walked along, Addie gazed up into the sky and thought of him, Samuel, the man who had loved her and Wesley, and she smiled. She knew she was blessed to have had him for a father. She was glad that both her sons bore his name: *Daniel Warren Coulter and Samuel Hiram Graham.*

When she reached her destination, she sat down and leaned her back against the great white oak, her and Hiram's "anniversary tree." Folding her arms to hug herself, she drew in a slow, deep breath and let it out. Then looking up through the branches, she laid her cares at the Savior's feet, whispering, "Father, hold me."

And her Heavenly Father did.

CHAPTER 25

He said unto them, Whosoever will come after me, let him deny
himself, and take up his cross, and follow me.

*—Mark 8:34 (*KJV*)*

The third building on Sparrow Street was a two-story, frame boardinghouse with a restaurant inside called the Preacher's House, owned and run by a man named John-Ott Owens and his wife, Leah. Sassie had worked there as a cook for nearly four years, mainly in an open-air cookhouse set beneath a spreading oak in the yard behind the establishment.

After work on this particular afternoon, with a wide-brimmed straw hat on her head and a small, wicker basket swinging on one arm, she strolled through the alley toward Main Street, headed for the mercantile. It had been on her mind all day to stop by there to look for a remnant of material to make Star a new dress for church.

As she came out of the alley, the afternoon sunlight hit her face. It had rained earlier, and the air smelled of wet grass and summertime; the ground was sprinkled with the petals of a tung oil tree. Then suddenly, she saw *them*— the Tuckers. *Maybe*, she told herself, *they won't notice me.* She didn't stop or even look their way, but when she heard Junior clear his throat and spit, she knew that she'd been spotted. Out of the corner of her eye, she saw Talmage toss his cigarette to the ground and start across the street in her direction. She looked around, but much to her dismay, the street was empty of activity; there didn't seem to be another soul milling about.

Just as she was about to mount the bottom step to the boardwalk, Talmage jumped in front of her, the heels of his boots thudding loudly on the planks. Sassie stepped to one side in an attempt to get past him, but he moved with her, blocking her way. His hair was long, hanging well past his collar, and greasy. His clothes smelled of smoke and sweat, and his breath stunk. It reminded Sassie of the smell given off by something dead.

His eyes roving over her face and body, he said, "I done told you one time—the sidewalk's fer whites. Darkies keep to the road." Like all white trash, he thought himself superior to blacks.

Behind her, Junior snickered. Although he was four years younger than Talmage, he was every bit as mean. She could almost feel his smirk burrowing into her back. Glancing down at the muddy street, she muttered something under her breath that sounded something like, "Pigs like yaw."

"What's that you sayin'?" Talmage asked.

"I said I ain't scared of yaw." She looked him directly in the face, hoping her fear didn't show. "Now, step aside, an' let me pass."

Grinning at her stupidly, he ignored her request and continued his bullying. In one quick movement, he reached out and jerked the basket off her arm and opened the lid. "Let's see what you've got in here." Inside, there was a small, drawstring bag containing two dollars in coins. He flipped a nickel into the air and caught it in his hand. "Tell me, who'd you steal this money from?"

She held his stare, her face expressionless. "I reckon I stole it from yo' mama," she said.

The insult stuck to his face. "Boy, you got a mouth on you, don't ya? Fi'ty years ago, that kind o' talk right there, out o' one o' yer kind would-a got yer hide busted, or got you sold off."

Sassie's gaze drifted toward the courthouse on the far end of the street, the national flag waving gently against the sky. "Not no more, though," she said softly.

"Give her belongings back an' step aside now—an' there'll be no trouble!"

Taken by surprise, Talmage wheeled around and found himself face-to-face with Daniel, who had suddenly and unexpectedly emerged from the drugstore. And judging by the look on his face, he had seen and heard more than enough to be thoroughly riled with the situation before him. Carson and Samuel tailed him closely, each holding a bottle of the popular soda water now being sold in town, made by Coca-Cola.

With a look of mild amusement, Talmage replied insolently, "Tell *you* what: *you* walk away now, an' there'll be no trouble. This here ain't none o' yer bis'ness."

"It is now," Daniel replied, "an' I say apologize." Sassie was looking at him miserably.

"What you gone do when I don't?" Talmage asked. When Daniel didn't answer him immediately, he smiled wanly and jeered. "Jus' what I figured—not a cotton-pickin' thang."

Instead of replying to the thug's remarks, Daniel looked at Sassie and said, "Take Carson and Samuel an' go to the feed store. Hiram's down there."

Relieved and grateful, she brushed past Talmage and guided the boys down the boardwalk hurriedly.

After watching her go, Talmage turned back to Daniel. "*Idea* you standin' there takin' the side of a sorry, high-yeller against two white men!" He shook his head as though that was so far beyond reason there was no possibility of anyone truly thinking that way.

"Don't see no men," Daniel replied. His tone had grown flat. "Just two ignorant fools. An' for your information, that nice young lady goin' yonder just happens to be my half sister."

Talmage slapped his thigh. "Yer *sister*! Why, do pardon! That case, I reckon it'd be your *mama* who's the sorry un! Any white woman who'd lay with a—"

Daniel gave no warning. He dove on Talmage, bearing him to the ground. The two rolled and struggled, each striving to overpower the other. Daniel hadn't been in a fight in years—not since having to defend himself against Alfred—but he managed to straddle Talmage and land a few solid blows to his head. Talmage thrashed and kicked, like a wild horse trying to buck free of his rider. They were a pretty even match until Junior attacked from behind and began dealing blows to Daniel's back, both men beating him pitilessly, until he could fight no more. All happened within minutes, and when it was over, the brothers slipped down the deserted alley and were gone, disappearing like smoke on the wind.

Daniel lay unmoving, his eyes closed, his thoughts disordered. *I'm tired of fightin', God.* No. That wasn't quite right, he told himself. *I'm tired of fightin' God.* That was it. He was tired of fighting God. Daniel knew he was saved. He had made a profession of faith years before and had been baptized; he was a member of the church, in good standing. He had even forgiven Alfred for all the torment he'd put them through, once he understood there was no correlation between being submissive to God and submitting to evildoers. And yet still, he felt wrenched apart, and he knew why. For months, he had been fighting God, arguing with Him, running from Him. And because of that, for months, he had known no real peace.

"Get up!"

Daniel had finally come to grips with the fact that he couldn't outrun God, or hide from Him. This time when the voice came to him, he didn't turn away, he didn't resist. Instead, he gave himself up, fully and wholly, surrendering his all to Him. At first he only mouthed the words, but then they came audibly. "Yes, Lord—yes, yes." As he lay there in total submission, he felt the wall he'd built around his heart crumble and fall like the walls of Jericho. He felt an outflowing of resistance, and an inflowing of the Holy Spirit. It was as though he was emptied out and filled up all at the same time. Wave upon wave, inexplicable relief and joy washed through him, filling his soul with a glorious sense of resolve and exultation. It was a feeling unlike anything Daniel had ever felt before. Though his body was battered and tired, deep inside, he felt rejuvenated and new, exuberant almost.

Ten minutes later, Hiram found him lying in a heap in the middle of the alley. His shirt was torn, his face was bloody, and he was covered with mud from head to toe. His assailants were nowhere in sight.

"What in...!" Hiram raced to Daniel's side and began shaking him gently, his first thought being that Daniel was out cold. He hollered, "Sassie, run get the doctor—and the sheriff!"

But Daniel opened his eyes and spoke, stopping her. "No!" He struggled to sit up, but the effort was too great. His ears were ringing, and he could hardly breathe. It felt like there was a branding iron pressing against his ribs. "I'm all right...I'm all right... just help me...help me up." He could hardly get the words out.

Hiram stared at him, thinking he must be dazed from the blows to his head. "Man, you don't look all right. You've been beat a sight. Them that did this to you need to be arrested an' thrown in jail."

Sassie glanced from one to the other, not knowing what to do. Awed by the sight of blood, Carson and Samuel were staring at Daniel as fixedly as a starving man might gaze upon food.

But Daniel shook his head. He was adamant. "No! There ain't no use in that...just let 'em go." Then he muttered something that really sounded insane. "It was the Lord...ain't a doubt in my mind...the Lord sent 'em to beat some sense into me." It didn't seem like such a far-fetched idea to him, considering the fact that He'd sent a fish to swallow up Jonah.

As he slumped against Hiram recovering his wind, Daniel looked up at the sky. It was calm and unclouded, a vast sea of blue that seemed to stretch on forever. Suddenly, part of a verse from the book of Jonah came to him: "*...and the sea ceased from her raging...*" He was unbelievably stiff and sore, but the constant storm within him had, at long last, ceased its raging. At long last, he knew and accepted God's purpose for his life.

At long last, his heart knew peace.

The following Sunday when the invitational was given, Daniel didn't hesitate. Even before Maude struck the first chords of the song, he had already stepped out and was headed to the front of the church, eager to share with the whole congregation that, in obedience to God's calling, he had surrendered to preach the gospel.

CHAPTER 26

Let Thy mercy, O Lord, be upon us, according as we hope in Thee.

Psalms 33:22 (KJV)

*J*t was the time of the year when folks tended the plants that grew from the seeds they had sown in spring. Midafternoon, Addie looked up from her flower bed to see a buggy turn off Longview Road onto the carriageway. Shading her eyes with one hand, she watched it approach and come to a stop at the front of the house. The driver hopped down, going quickly to the other side to assist his passenger. Addie stood up and removed her gloves as the woman proceeded toward her, looking about curiously. Addie waited, wondering what this person might want.

She was an older, attractive woman, with graying hair and straight shoulders, her figure still lean. She was the first to speak, saying, "How do you do?" as she came toward Addie. The two women eyed each other with interest.

"Good afternoon," Addie replied. She met the woman's gaze directly, immediately noticing her lovely eyes. They were cornflower blue, and there was something about them that seemed hauntingly familiar.

"I'm Charlotte...Charlotte Adams," the woman said. Her eyes never left Addie's face.

Trying to place where she'd heard that name before, Addie smiled and said, "Pleased to meet you, Mrs. Adams. I'm Addie Graham." She was aware that the woman was staring at her, rather studying her, intensely. She seemed very pensive. It was strange, very odd. And the oddest thing was that she seemed so familiar to her. *It's her eyes,* Addie thought.

"Addie," the woman repeated. "What a beautiful name. My mother's name was Adeline." Her voice sounded almost sad as she said it.

Without knowing why, Addie suddenly felt pressed upon to say, "My mother's name was Rachel."

Upon hearing this, Charlotte extended her hands toward Addie, and Addie took them, inspirited by an unexplainable feeling of warmth for the woman. Something within tugged at her. "Have we met somewhere before?" she asked. She had a strong sense they had; the uncertainty of it nagged her as she tried to place her in her mind.

The answer was slow in coming. "No. I'm certain we haven't... My maiden name was Davis." Blinking fast, Charlotte's eyes searched Addie's face as she said it.

Addie felt her heart jump. Of course! Those eyes! How well she knew them! They were the same as Wesley's. And Emily's. *And mine.* Looking into them was like looking into her own eyes. There was no doubt in her mind that she and this Charlotte Adams were somehow related. *Through my father,* she thought. Suddenly, she could hardly breathe. The realization was so overwhelming it made her feel weak. *But...* She couldn't begin to imagine how she had found her, or why she had come.

Tears spilled onto Addie's cheeks, and there were tears on Charlotte's face as well, acknowledging the truth they both knew. A sweet mingling of roses and tilled earth rose up and surrounded them. Charlotte's voice trembled as she said, "You have a brother...is he...?"

Addie managed to catch her breath and say, "Wesley...yes... he—he lives just down the road..."

Hearing that, Charlotte closed her eyes and took a deep breath, a feeling of infinite relief and joy flooding through her. She had been longing for this day—waiting for this moment— for such a long time. She had never stopped praying, never given up hope of locating her brother's children—*Dalton's* children; and now, she and his daughter had finally come together, face-to-face. It was a miracle. She opened her eyes again then and looked at Addie, her face flushed with happiness. She took a few moments to collect herself before saying, "I always knew the Lord would someday lead me to you, my dear niece."

Just then, the front door opened, and Hiram came down the steps. Surprised to see her, he asked, "Why, Mrs. Adams, what brings you this way?"

Over the next couple of hours, the mystery began to unravel. Charlotte and Claudia had been at the Alice Hotel in Ellisville last Thursday afternoon, Charlotte explained, eating peach pie à la mode, like they do every Thursday. She was right in the middle of telling Claudia how she would give just about anything to have one of Mr. Henry Ford's newfangled cars. Pausing, she looked around the room at everyone and said, "I told her it would do us old girls a world of good to run around the countryside without a saddle for once, just be free as the wind." Her eyes twinkled. Well, lo and behold who do you think came walking through the front door but Newt Knight! She had not seen or thought about that old sinner in years, and he was the last person she cared about seeing that day. But as it turned out, Charlotte said, he commenced to tell her a very interesting story.

Newt had told her about how he'd been in Oakdale four years ago, right at Christmastime, and how he'd stopped a man on the street to get directions to Collinsville. Charlotte looked at Wesley and smiled. "He said the man introduced himself as Wesley Warren, the son of Samuel and Rachel Warren, but that he knew, just by looking at you, that you were Dalton's boy."

Charlotte looked around at all of them then—her niece and nephew, great-nieces, great-nephews— and she couldn't help but think about the power that had unified them, what a great gift God had bestowed upon them. She had not felt this blessed or been this happy in years, decades.

There was so much they wanted to talk about, so much they wanted to find out about one another, but they had several lifetimes to cover, and the day, which had turned out to be one of the best days of their lives, was quickly slipping past. Charlotte could hardly bring herself to leave, but she had to if she was to get home before dark. She promised to come back soon, perhaps the following week, and she invited everyone to come visit her at her home. She could hardly wait to tell Claudia what had happened.

Before she climbed into the buggy, she suddenly remembered something. To Wesley and Addie, she said, "Now that I've found y'all, I'll go to the bank next week and have Dalton's part of my parents' estate converted into drafts for each of you."

EPILOGUE

*J*t was a pleasant day, not a cloud in the sky, and a good day for fishing. Jesse and Wiley Parker were at a table in the side yard, sleeves rolled up, cleaning the white perch they had caught from the Parkers' pond.

When Jesse finished scaling the fish he was working on, he dropped it into a pan of fresh water and reached for another. "This is that big 'un that almost broke my line," Addie heard him say.

"Looks like they were biting today," she said as she walked up.

"Hey, Aunt Addie." Jesse smiled that quick boyish grin of his and proceeded to lay it on thick. "Yes, ma'am, you can say that again! We had to hide behind a tree just so's to bait our hooks!"

Addie chuckled and then asked, "Where's your mama? I need to talk to her about tomorrow's picnic."

Jesse pointed with his knife. "She's in yonder, in the house."

"Well, soon as y'all get those fish cooked, give me a holler."

Birds were singing; the afternoon sun streamed through the trees. Leaves were beginning to turn golden, and the gentlest whisper of a breeze ruffled them in such a way one might wonder if God himself was sitting amid the branches, breathing. It was early October, and a perfect day for a picnic.

Tables and chairs were moved outside from house to yard; the men had dug a barbeque pit and grilled several chickens over hickory coals, and the women had handled the rest. Unable to eat another bite, Hiram went and sat down on an old quilt in the shade; he leaned his head against the trunk of the oak, with intentions of stretching out for a nap. Having seen him so settled, Addie soon joined him there. He put an arm around her naturally and pulled her close; she laid her head on her husband's shoulder, and for a while they rested.

When Hiram heard her giggle, he opened one eye and asked, "What's so funny?"

Smiling, yet not trying to make a joke of it, she looked up at him and gave up what she had been pondering. "It's not really so much *funny*," she said, "but as I sat here, I just couldn't help thinking: Here I am, the daughter of an unlawful renegade hanged by the army, married first to a man who was a rapist and murderer who killed my own, poor mama! And *you*, fine sir, the brother of a cold-blooded killer who's serving a life sentence for murdering your brother-in-law's sister-in-law! Now, without a doubt, *surely* you have to agree, we've got ourselves some kind of family!" Set against traditional standards, theirs had ever possessed a rather complex and scandalous history. For, as bad as those things were, it was nowhere near the all of it.

Before making a comment on what she'd said, for a moment Hiram sat looking around quietly. There was twenty of them present altogether: Wesley, his head down on the table, was counting aloud as the younger ones – Meggie, Carson, Rachel, Samuel, and Ellis – ran about squealing as they started a game of hide-and-seek. Asher, Daniel, Obie, and Jesse had set up the checkerboard on a stump. Laura, Penelope, Charlotte, Amelia, and Sassie had abandoned the dishes and were rocking back and forth on the front porch, laughing. Penelope's baby was due in the spring, around the same time Julie Robertson was expecting. Star and Nora were chasing after a cat, shrieking loudly, their starched pinafores billowing in the breeze. It made him smile to watch them. Even Libby was part of it all, having recovered the mind she'd almost lost.

Hiram thought of Emily, away at the university in Hattiesburg, pursuing her dream, and, Travis and Abigail, Sarah Beth and Jonathan, miles north of there, in Memphis. He found himself remembering some of their forebears, some of those who had passed on—Stell, Claire, Creenie, Bonnie, Anna—and what each of them, faults alloyed, had meant to all the others. They, every one, were still there, in their hearts.

It was to Hiram a sobering vision, one he beheld preciously. One that reminded him that despite life's inevitable trials and disappointments, all the hard times and tragedies, the Lord truly had smiled upon them all, each and every one—and especially him. The day, the blessings, the bounty, the love—it all seemed as close to Heaven as he could imagine. Suddenly, he felt surrounded by nothing but peace and contentment, surrounded by those he loved most in the world, and by those who loved him.

And, most important of all, right there beside him was Addie. His beloved Addie. She was his heart's companion. With her, he felt a love and passion he had never felt before. She had made him a better man than he really was, a man he had never been before he met her. He thought about the life they shared…the children they loved…It was amazing how fast ten years had passed. Suddenly, his throat felt tight with unexpected emotion. He felt blessed beyond measure.

Rendered momentarily speechless, he drew Addie evermore close. Finally, when he had regained his composure, he drawled softly, "Well, I hadn't ever thought about it exactly like that before, but, yes, ma'am, without a doubt I'd have to say we do indeed have ourselves some kind of family."

Some kind of fine and wonderful family.

THE END

AUTHOR'S NOTE

*A*s far back as biblical times, the preparation of food and the breaking of bread together have held a significant place in the lives of people the world over. At most any occasion we celebrate, whether happy or sad, there seems to be an inseparable association between food and fellowship, food and friendship, food and hospitality, even food and love.

I had not realized how much I talked about food in the "story about love" trilogy until the meals described in the books became a regular point of discussion at signing events, reading club meetings, etc.—and until it was suggested that I include recipes for the dishes mentioned at the end of *An Unclouded Day*. I quickly discovered, however, to do so would entail writing an entire cookbook. (Hmmm…)

So instead, I've shared a few of those most frequently requested:

CLAIRE'S TEA CAKES

4 c. all-purpose flour
2 eggs
1 tsp. baking soda
1/2 c. buttermilk
2 tsp. baking powder
2 sticks of butter, softened
2 c. white sugar
1 tsp. vanilla

Preheat oven to 350 degrees. Sift together flour, baking soda, and baking powder.

Add remaining ingredients and mix well. Dough should be soft. Roll out on floured surface to 1/4-inch thick. Cut into desired shapes and bake on a greased cookie sheet 10–12 minutes. *If desired, dust lightly with powdered sugar.

SUGARED PECANS

4–5 c. pecan halves
1 stick butter
1 1/2 c. brown sugar

Preheat oven to 325 degrees. Melt butter and add brown sugar, stirring until sugar is dissolved. Add pecans. Stir until pecans are completely coated. Turn out onto an ungreased cookie sheet, spreading so that pecans are in one layer. Bake for 25–30 minutes, stirring every 5 minutes, until pecans are toasted. Let cool completely.

ADDIE'S SWEET POTATO CASSEROLE

3 c. cooked sweet potatoes
1/2 stick butter
1 c. white sugar
1/2 c. milk
½ tsp. salt
1 tsp. vanilla
2 eggs, beaten
Topping:
1 c. brown sugar
1/2 stick butter
1/2 c. flour
1 c. chopped pecans

Mix mashed potatoes, sugar, salt, eggs, 1/2 stick butter, milk, and vanilla. Pour into a casserole dish. Combine brown sugar and flour, add 1/2 stick butter and mix together with a fork. Add pecans and stir. Pour topping mixture over potato mixture. Bake at 350 degrees for 35 minutes.

SASSIE'S SKILLET APPLE PIE

4 lb. Granny Smith apples
1 tsp. cinnamon
3/4 c. white sugar
1/2 c. butter
1 c. light brown sugar
2 piecrusts
1 egg white
2 tbs. white sugar

Preheat oven to 350 degrees. Peel apples and cut into 1/2-inch-thick pieces. Toss apples with cinnamon and white sugar. Melt butter in a 10-inch cast-iron skillet; add brown sugar and cook, stirring constantly 1 or 2 minutes or until sugar is dissolved. Remove from heat and lay bottom piecrust in skillet over butter/sugar mixture. Pour apples into piecrust and top with second piecrust. Whisk egg white until foamy and brush top piecrust with it. Sprinkle with 2 tablespoon white sugar. Bake for 1 hour to 1 hour 10 minutes, until piecrust is golden brown. Delicious served with ice cream.

Note: For blackberry pie: Substitute 4 cups blackberries for apples. Omit cinnamon.

CLAUDIA'S LEMON MERINGUE PIE

1 c. sugar
1 1/4 cups water
1 tbs. butter

Heat these three ingredients until sugar dissolves.

Mix together 4 tablespoon cornstarch and 3 tablespoon cold water. Add to sugar mixture.

Cook over medium heat until mixture is clear, about 8 minutes.

Add 4 tablespoon lemon juice and 2 teaspoon lemon zest. Cook 2 minutes longer.

Beat 3 egg yolks with 2 tablespoon milk. Gradually stir about a cup of hot mixture into egg yolks, then return to pan and bring to a gentle boil. Cook, stirring constantly, about 2 minutes. Pour into baked pie crust. Top with Meringue and bake at 350 degrees for 12–15 minutes until meringue is golden.

Meringue:

3 egg whites

6 tbs. sugar
1 tsp. lemon juice

Beat egg whites until soft peaks form. Add lemon juice and gradually add sugar and beat until stiff peaks form, 4 or 5 minutes. Spread over pie and bake.

Note: For a more generous meringue, 4 egg whites can be used.

LAURA'S COCONUT PIE

1 c. sugar
1/2 stick butter
2 heaping tbs. plain flour
1 tsp. vanilla
3 eggs, separated
1/2 tsp. coconut flavoring, optional
2 c. milk
1 c. flaked coconut

Mix together flour and sugar. Mix in beaten egg yolks. Stir in milk. Cook, stirring, until thick and bubbly. Add butter and vanilla. Cook about 2 minutes longer. Stir in coconut. Pour hot filling into baked piecrust. Top with meringue (below). Sprinkle 1/3 cup coconut over meringue and bake at 350 degrees for 12–15 minutes until golden.

Meringue: Beat egg whites until soft peaks form. Gradually beat in 3 tablespoons sugar until stiff peaks form. Spread pie and bake until golden.

Note: For chocolate pie: Omit coconut and coconut flavoring. Add 3 tablespoon cocoa.

POUND CAKE

2 sticks oleo
3 c. plain flour
1/2 c. Crisco
3 c. sugar
8 oz. cream cheese
1 tsp. vanilla
6 eggs

Cream together oleo, Crisco, cream cheese, sugar, and vanilla. Add eggs, 2 at a time, alternating with 1 cup of flour at a time. Turn batter into pan. Place in cold oven; bake at 300 degrees for 1 hour and 45 minutes. Do not open oven during baking.

SCRATCH BROWNIES

2 sticks butter
4 eggs
2 c. sugar
2/3 c. cocoa
2 tsp. vanilla
1 c. self-rising flour
1 c. chopped pecans or walnuts (optional)

Beat butter, sugar, eggs, and vanilla until fluffy. Add dry ingredients and mix together well. Stir in nuts. Turn and spread batter evenly into a greased baking dish. Bake at 325 degrees for 30–35 minutes. Let cool. Glaze. Cut into bars.

Glaze: Mix together ¼ cup softened butter, ¼ cup milk, ¼ cup cocoa, 3 cups powdered sugar, and a dash of salt. Spread over cooled brownies.

CHARLOTTE'S FAVORITE PEACH PIE A LA MODE

6 medium peaches, peeled and sliced
5 slices white bread, crust removed
1 – 1 ½ cups sugar
2 T all-purpose flour
1 egg
½ cup butter, melted

Preheat oven 350 degrees. Place peaches in a lightly greased 8-inch square baking dish. Cut bread into strips and arrange evenly over peaches. Mix together: sugar, flour, egg, and butter. Pour over bread and peaches. Bake 35 minutes, or until golden brown. Serve with vanilla ice cream.